Blood on Snow

BLOOD ON SNOW

JO NESBØ

Translated from the Norwegian by **Neil Smith**

RANDOM HOUSE
LARGE PRINT

English translation copyright © 2015 by Neil Smith

All rights reserved.
Published in the United States of America by Random House Large Print in association with Alfred A. Knopf, New York.
Distributed by Random House LLC, New York, a Penguin Random House Company. Originally published in Norway as **Blod på Snø** by H. Aschehough & Co. (W. Nygaard), Oslo, 2015. Copyright © 2015 by Jo Nesbø. This translation was simultaneously published in Great Britain by Harvill Secker, an imprint of Random House Group Ltd., London.

Cover design by Peter Mendelsund

The Library of Congress has established a Cataloging-in-Publication record for this title.

ISBN: 978-0-8041-9488-4

www.randomhouse.com/largeprint

FIRST LARGE PRINT EDITION

Printed in the United States of America
10 9 8 7 6 5 4 3 2 1

This Large Print edition published in accord with the standards of the N.A.V.H.

Blood on Snow

CHAPTER 1

The snow was dancing like cotton wool in the light of the street lamps. Aimlessly, unable to decide whether it wanted to fall up or down, just letting itself be driven by the hellish, ice-cold wind that was sweeping in from the great darkness covering the Oslo fjord. Together they swirled, wind and snow, round and round in the darkness between the warehouses on the quayside that were all shut for the night. Until the wind got fed up and dumped its dance partner beside the wall. And there the dry, windswept snow was settling around the shoes of the man I had just shot in the chest and neck.

Blood was dripping down onto the snow from the bottom of his shirt. I don't actually know a lot about snow—or much else, for that matter—but I've read that snow crystals formed when it's really cold are completely different from wet snow, heavy flakes, or the crunchy stuff. That it's the shape of the crystals and the dryness of the snow that make the haemoglobin in the blood retain that deep red colour. Either way, the snow under him made me think of a king's robe, all purple and lined with ermine, like the drawings in the book of Norwegian folk tales my mother used to read to me. She liked fairy tales and kings. That's probably why she named me after a king.

The **Evening Post** had said that if the cold carried on like this until New Year, 1977 would be the coldest year since the war, and that we'd remember it as the start of the new ice age scientists had been predicting for a while. But what did I know? All I knew was that the man standing in front of me would soon be dead. There was no mistaking the way his body was shaking. He was one of the Fisherman's men. It was nothing personal. I told him as much before he collapsed, leaving a smear of blood down the wall. If I ever get shot, I'd rather it was personal. I didn't say it to stop his ghost coming after me—I don't believe in ghosts. I just couldn't think of anything else to say. Obviously I could have just kept my mouth shut. That's what I usually do, after all. So there must have been something that made me so talkative all of a sudden. Maybe it was because there were only a few days to go before Christmas. I've heard that people are supposed to feel closer to each other around Christmas. But what do I know?

I thought the blood would freeze on top of the snow and end up just lying there. But instead the snow sucked the blood up as it fell, drawing it in under the surface, hiding it, as if it had some sort

of use for it. As I walked home I imagined a snowman rising up from the snowdrift, one with clearly
visible veins of blood under its deathly pale skin
of ice.

On the way back to my flat I called Daniel Hoffmann from a phone box to tell him the job was
done.

Hoffmann said that was good. As usual, he didn't
ask any questions. Either he'd learned to trust me
in the course of the four years I'd been working as
a fixer for him, or else he didn't actually want to
know. The job was done, so why would a man like
him trouble himself with that sort of thing when
what he was paying for was to have fewer problems? Hoffmann asked me to go down to the office
the next day—he said he had a new job for me.

"A new job?" I asked, feeling my heart skip a beat.

"Yes," Hoffmann said. "As in a new commis-
sion."

"Oh, okay."

I hung up, relieved. I don't really do much more
than commissions. I can't actually be used for much
more than that.

Here are four things I can't be used for. Driving
a getaway car. I can drive fast, that's fine. But I can't
drive inconspicuously, and anyone driving a getaway car has to be able to do both. They have to
be able to drive so they look just like any other car
on the road. I landed myself and two other men
in prison because I can't drive inconspicuously

enough. I drove like a demon, switching between forest tracks and main roads, and I'd long since lost our pursuers, and was just a few kilometres from the Swedish border. I slowed down and drove in a steady, law-abiding way like a grandad on a Sunday outing. And we still got stopped by a police patrol. They said afterwards that they had no idea it was the car used in the robbery, and that I hadn't been driving too fast or breaking any of the rules of the road. They said it was the **way** I was driving. I've no idea what they meant, but they said it was suspicious.

I can't be used in robberies. I've read that more than half of all bank employees who experience a robbery end up with psychological problems afterwards, some of them for the rest of their lives. I don't know why, but the old man who was behind the counter of the post office when we went in was in a big hurry to develop psychological problems. He fell to pieces just because the barrel of my shotgun was pointed in his general direction, apparently. I saw in the paper the next day that he was suffering from psychological problems. Not much of a diagnosis, but either way, if there's one thing you don't want, it's psychological problems. So I went to visit him in hospital. Obviously he didn't recognise me—I'd been wearing a Santa Claus mask in the post office. (It was the perfect disguise. No one gave a second glance to three lads in Santa Claus outfits carrying sacks as they ran out of a post office

in the middle of the Christmas shopping crowds.)
I stopped in the doorway to the ward and looked
at the old man. He was reading **Class Struggle,** the
Communist newspaper. Not that I've got anything
against Communists as individuals. Okay, maybe
I have. But I don't **want** to have anything against
them as individuals, I just think they're wrong. So I
felt a bit guilty when I realised that I felt a lot better
because the guy was reading **Class Struggle.** But
obviously there's a big difference between feeling
a bit guilty and a lot guilty. And like I said, I felt a
lot better. But I stopped doing robberies. After all,
there was no guarantee the next one would be a
Communist.

And I can't work with drugs, that's number three.
I just can't do it. It's not that I can't get money out
of people who are in debt to my employers. Junkies
only have themselves to blame, and in my opin-
ion people should pay for their mistakes, plain and
simple. The problem's more that I have a weak,
sensitive nature, as my mum once put it. I suppose
she saw herself in me. Either way, I have to stay well
away from drugs. Like her, I'm the sort of person
who's just looking for someone to submit to. Reli-
gion, a big-brother figure, a boss. Drink and drugs.
Besides, I can't do math either, I can hardly count
to ten without losing my concentration. Which is
kind of stupid if you're going to sell drugs or collect
debts—that ought to be pretty obvious.

Okay. Last one. Prostitution. Same sort of thing

there. I don't have a problem with women earning money whatever way they like, and the idea
that a guy—me, for instance—should get a third
of the money for sorting things out so the women
can concentrate on the actual work. A good pimp
is worth every krone they pay him, I've always
thought that. The problem is that I fall in love so
quickly, and then I stop seeing it in terms of business. And I can't handle shaking, hitting or threat-
ening the women, whether or not I'm in love with
them. Something to do with my mother, maybe,
what do I know? That's probably why I can't stand
seeing other people beating up women either.
Something just snaps. Take Maria, for instance.
Deaf and dumb, with a limp. I don't know what
those two things have got to do with each other—
nothing probably—but it's a bit like once you start
getting bad cards, they just keep coming. Which
is probably why Maria ended up with an idiot
junkie boyfriend as well. He had a fancy French
name, Myriel, but owed Hoffmann thirteen thousand for drugs. The first time I saw her was when
Pine, Hoffmann's head pimp, pointed out a girl in
a home-made coat and with her hair up in a bun,
looking like she'd just left church. She was sitting on
the steps in front of Ridderhallen, crying, and Pine
told me she was going to have to pay back her boyfriend's drug debt in kind. I thought it best to give
her a gentle start, just hand-jobs. But she jumped

out of the first car she got into after barely ten seconds. She stood there in floods of tears while Pine yelled at her. Maybe he thought she'd hear him if he shouted loud enough. Maybe that was what did it. The yelling. And my mum. Either way, something snapped, and even if I could see what Pine was trying to get into her head by the use of very loud sound waves, I ended up decking him, my own boss. Then I took Maria to a flat I knew was empty, then went to tell Hoffmann that I was no use as a pimp either.

But Hoffmann said—and I had to agree with him—that he couldn't let people get away without paying their debts, because that sort of thing soon spreads to other, more important customers. So, well aware that Pine and Hoffmann were after the girl because she'd been stupid enough to take on her boyfriend's debts, I went out looking until I found the Frenchman in a squat up in Fagerborg. He was both wrecked by drugs and broke, so I realised I wasn't going to get a single krone out of him, no matter how much I shook him. I said that if he so much as approached Maria again I'd smash his nose into his brain. To be honest, I'm not sure there was much left of either of them. So I went back to Hoffmann, said the boyfriend had managed to get hold of some money, handed him thirteen thousand and said I presumed that meant hunting season on the girl was over.

I don't know if Maria had been a user while they were together, if she was the sort who looked for ways to be submissive, but she seemed pretty straight now, at least. She worked in a small supermarket, and I looked in every now and then to make sure things were okay, and that her junkie boyfriend hadn't popped up to ruin things for her again. Obviously I made sure she couldn't see me, just stood outside in the darkness looking into the well-lit shop, watching her sitting at the till, putting things in bags, and pointing at one of the others if anyone spoke to her. Every so often I suppose we all need to feel that we're living up to our parents. I don't know what Dad had that I could live up to—this is probably more about Mum. She was better at looking after other people than herself, and I suppose I saw that as a kind of ideal back then. God knows. Either way, I didn't really have much use for the money I was earning from Hoffmann. So what if I dealt a decent card to a girl who'd been given such a lousy hand?

Anyway. To sum up, let's put it like this: I'm no good at driving slowly, I'm way too soft, I fall in love far too easily, I lose my head when I get angry, and I'm bad at math. I've read a bit, but I don't really know much, and certainly nothing anyone would find useful. And stalactites grow faster than I can write.

So what on earth can a man like Daniel Hoffmann use someone like me for?

The answer is—as you might have worked out already—as a fixer.

I don't have to drive, and I mostly kill the sort of men who deserve it, and the numbers aren't exactly hard to keep track of. Not right now, anyway.

There are two calculations.

To start with, there's the one that's ticking away the whole time: When exactly do you reach the point where you know so much about your boss that he starts to get worried? And when do you know he's beginning to wonder if he ought to fix the fixer? Like one of those black widows. Not that I know much about arachnology or whatever it's called, but I think the widows let the males, who are much smaller, fuck them. Then, when he's finished and the female has no more use for him, she eats him. In **Animal Kingdom 4: Insects and Spiders** in the Deichman Library there's a picture of a black widow with the male's chewed-off pedipalp, which is like the spider's cock, still hanging from her genitals. And you can see the blood-red, hourglass-shaped mark on the female's abdomen. Because the hourglass is running, you pathetic, randy little male spider, and you need to keep to your allotted visiting time. Or, to be more accurate, you need to know when visiting time is over. And then you get the fuck out of there, come what may, with a couple of bullets in the side or whatever— you just have to get away, to the only thing that can save you.

Blood on Snow

That's how I saw it. Do what you have to, but don't get too close.

And that's why I was seriously fucking worried about the new job Hoffmann had given me.

He wanted me to fix his wife.

CHAPTER 2

I want you to make it look like a break-in,
Olav."

"Why?" I asked.

"Because it needs to look like something else,
Olav, not what it really is. The police always get
upset when civilians are killed. They put a little too
much effort into their investigation. And when a
woman who has a lover is found dead, everything
points to her husband. Obviously, in ninety per
cent of cases this is perfectly justified."

"Seventy-four, sir."

"Sorry?"

"Just something I read, sir."

Okay, we don't usually call people "sir" in Norway, no matter how superior they are. With the
exception of the royal family, of course, who are
addressed as Your Royal Highness. Daniel Hoffmann would probably have preferred that. The title
of "sir" was something Hoffmann had imported
from England, together with his leather furniture,

red mahogany bookcases and leather-bound books full of the old, yellowing, unread pages of what were presumably English classics. But how should I know, I only recognised the usual names: Dickens, Brontë, Austen. Either way, the dead authors made the air in his office so dry that I always ended up coughing a fine spray of lung cells long after my visits. I don't know what it was about England that fascinated Hoffmann, but I knew he'd spent a short time there as a student, and came home with his case stuffed full of tweed suits, ambition and an affected Oxford English with a Norwegian twang. No degree or certificates, just a belief that money is everything. And that if you're going to succeed in business, you have to concentrate on markets where the competition is weakest. Which in Oslo at that time meant prostitution. I think his analysis really was that simple. Daniel Hoffmann had worked out that in a market run by charlatans, idiots and amateurs, even a distinctly average man could end up king of the castle. It was just a matter of having the necessary moral flexibility required to recruit and send girls out into prostitution on a daily basis. And, after giving the matter due consideration, Daniel Hoffmann concluded that he did. When he expanded his business into the heroin market a few years later, Hoffmann was already a man who regarded himself as a success. And since the heroin market in Oslo up to then had been run by jokers, idiots and amateurs, as well as junkies, and since it turned out that Hoffmann also possessed sufficient moral flexibility to despatch people into a narcotic hell, this became another success. The only problem that Hoffmann now faced was the Fisherman. The Fisherman was a fairly recent competitor in the heroin market, and, as it turned out, he was no idiot. God knows, there were enough addicts in Oslo for both of them, but they were each trying their best to wipe the other off the face of the earth. Why? Well, I assume that neither of them was born with my innate talent for subordination. And things get a bit messy when people like that, who **have** to be in charge, who **have** to sit on the throne, find out that their women are being unfaithful. I think the Daniel Hoffmanns of this world would have better and simpler lives if they could learn to look the other way, and maybe accept that their wives had an affair or two.

"I was thinking of taking a holiday over Christmas," I said. "Asking someone to come with me, and go away for a while."

"A travelling companion? I didn't think you knew anyone that intimately, Olav? That's one of the things I like about you, you know. That you haven't got anyone to tell secrets to." He smiled and tapped the ash from his cigar. I didn't get upset—he meant well. The word "Cohiba" was printed on the cigar band. I read somewhere that at the turn of the century cigars were the most common Christmas present in the Western Hemisphere. Would that be a good idea? I didn't even know if she smoked. I hadn't seen her smoking at work, anyway.

"I haven't asked yet," I said. "But—"

"I'll pay you five times your usual fee," Hoffmann said. "So you can take the person in question on a never-ending Christmas holiday afterwards if you want."

I tried to do the math. But like I said, I'm pretty useless.

"Here's the address," Hoffmann said.

I had worked for him for four years without knowing where he lived. But then, why should I have known? He didn't know where I lived. And I'd never met his new wife either, just heard Pine going on about how hot she was, and how much he'd be able to rake in if he had a bitch like that on the streets.

"She's on her own in the house most of the day," Hoffmann said. "At least that's what she tells me. Do it whatever way you like, Olav. I trust you. The least I know, the better. Understood?"

I nodded. The **less** I know, I thought.

"Olav?"

"Yes, sir, understood."

"Good."

"Let me think about it till tomorrow, sir."

Hoffmann raised one of his neatly manicured eyebrows. I don't know much about evolution and stuff like that, but didn't Darwin say there were only six universal facial expressions for human emotions? I've no idea if Hoffmann had six human emotions, but I think what he was hoping to communicate with his raised eyebrow—in contrast to what he would have meant by an open-mouthed stare—was mild annoyance combined with reflection and intelligence.

"I've just given you the details, Olav. And now—after that—you're thinking about **refusing**?"

The threat was barely audible. No, actually, if that was the case then I probably wouldn't have picked up on it. I'm completely tone-deaf when it comes to noticing the undertones and subtexts in what people say. So we can assume that the threat was obvious enough. Daniel Hoffmann had clear blue eyes and black eyelashes. If he was a girl I'd have said it was make-up. I don't know why I mention that, it's got nothing to do with anything.

"I didn't have time to respond before you gave me the details, sir," I said. "You'll have an answer by this evening, if that's okay, sir?"

He looked at me. Blew cigar smoke in my direction. I sat there with my hands in my lap. Fiddling with the brim of the labourer's cap I didn't actually have.

"By six," he said. "That's when I leave the office."

I nodded.

As I walked home along the city streets through the snowstorm, four o'clock came and darkness settled over the city again after just a few hours of grey daylight. The wind was still strong, and there was an unsettling whistling sound from dark corners. But like I said, I don't believe in ghosts. The snow crunched under the soles of my boots, like the snapping spines of dusty old books, but I was thinking. I usually try to avoid doing that. It's not an area where I see any hope of improvement with practice, and experience has taught me that it rarely leads to anything good. But I was back in the first of those two calculations. The fix itself ought to be fine. To be honest, it would be easier than the other jobs I had done. And the fact that she was going to die was fine as well: like I said, I think all of us—men and women alike—have to accept the consequences when we make mistakes. What worried me more was what was bound to happen afterwards. When I was the guy who had fixed Daniel Hoffmann's wife. The man who knew everything and had the power to determine Daniel Hoffmann's future once the police started their investigation. Power over someone who wasn't capable of subordination. And a man Hoffmann owed five times the usual fee. Why had he offered that for a job that was less complicated than normal?

I felt like I was sitting at a poker table with four heavily armed, innately suspicious bad losers. And I'd just managed to get a hand of four aces. Sometimes good news is so improbably good that it's bad.

Okay, so what a smart poker player would do here is get rid of the cards, soak up the loss and hope for better—and more appropriate—luck in the next round. My problem was that it was far too late to fold. I knew Hoffmann was going to be behind the murder of his wife, regardless of whether it was me or someone else who did it.

I realised where my steps had taken me, and stared into the light.

She had her hair pulled up in a bun, the way my mum used to. She was nodding and smiling at customers who spoke to her. Most of them probably knew she was deaf and dumb. Wishing her "Happy Christmas," thanking her. The typical pleasantries that people say to each other.

Five times the usual fee. A never-ending Christmas holiday.

CHAPTER 3

I rented a room in a small hotel right opposite the Hoffmanns' apartment in Bygdøy Allé.
The plan was to watch what the wife did for a couple of days, see if she went anywhere while her husband was at work, or if she had any visitors. Not
that I was interested in finding out who her lover
was. My aim was simply to work out the best, least
risky time to strike, when she was on her own at
home and wasn't likely to be disturbed.

The room turned out to be the perfect vantage
point not only to watch Corina Hoffmann coming
and going, but also to see what she got up to inside
the apartment. Evidently they never bothered to
close the curtains. Most people don't, in a city
where there's no sun to shut out, and people outside are more interested in getting into the warm
somewhere than they are in standing and staring.

For the first few hours I didn't see anyone in
there. Just a living room bathed in light. The Hoffmanns weren't exactly sparing with the electric-

ity. The furniture wasn't English; it looked more French, especially the strange sofa in the middle of the room that only had a back at one end. Presumably it was what the French call a **chaise longue** which—unless my French teacher was having me on—means "long chair." Ornate, asymmetrical carving, with some sort of nature-inspired upholstery. Rococo, according to my mum's art history books, but it could just as well have been knocked together by a local craftsman and painted in the traditional style out in the Norwegian countryside for all I knew. Either way, it wasn't the sort of furniture someone young would choose, so I guess it was Hoffmann's ex-wife's. Pine had said Hoffmann threw her out the year she turned fifty. **Because** she'd turned fifty. And because their son had moved out and she no longer filled any function in his home. And—according to Pine—he had said all this to her face, and she had accepted it. Along with a flat by the sea and a cheque for one and a half million kroner.

To pass the time I took out the sheets of paper I'd been writing on. It was really just a form of scribbling. Well, that's not quite true, I suppose it was more of a letter. A letter to someone whose identity I didn't know. Actually, maybe I did. But I'm not exactly much good at writing, so there were a lot of mistakes, a lot that had to be cut. To be honest, a lot of paper and ink had gone into every word that I'd kept. And things went so slowly this time that

Blood on Snow

I eventually just put the paper down, lit a cigarette and did some daydreaming instead.

Like I said, I'd never seen any member of Hoffmann's family, but I could see them in my mind's eye as I sat there looking into the apartment on the other side of the street. I liked looking in on other people. Always had done. So I did what I always did, and imagined family life in there. A nine-year-old son, home from school, sitting in the living room reading all the strange books he'd taken out from the library. The mother singing quietly to herself as she prepared dinner in the kitchen. The way mother and son tense for a moment when there's a noise from the door. Then how they suddenly relax when the man in the hall calls out "I'm home!" in a clear, cheerful voice, and they run out to greet him and give him a hug.

While I was sitting there immersed in happy thoughts, Corina Hoffmann walked into the living room from the bedroom, and everything changed.

The light.

The temperature.

The calculations.

That afternoon I didn't go to the supermarket.

I didn't wait for Maria the way I sometimes did, I didn't follow her to the underground at a safe distance, I didn't stand right behind her in the crowd in the middle of the train, where she always liked to stand even if there were empty seats. That afternoon I didn't stand there like a madman, whispering things to her that only I could hear.

That afternoon I sat bewitched in a darkened room, staring at the woman on the other side of the street. Corina Hoffmann. I could say whatever I wanted, as loudly as I wanted—there was no one to hear me. And I didn't have to look at her from behind, look at her hair so hard that I managed to see a beauty in it that wasn't actually there.

Tightrope-walker. That was the first thing I thought when Corina Hoffmann walked into the room. She was wearing a white terry-cloth dressing gown, and she moved like a cat. By that I don't mean that she ambled along like some mammals do, cats and camels, for instance. Moving both legs on one side before moving the others. Or so I've heard. What I mean is that cats—if I've got this right—walk on tiptoe, and that they put their back paws on the same spot as their front paws. That was what Corina was doing. Setting her naked feet down with her ankles straight, and putting the second foot down close to the first. Like a tightrope-walker.

Everything about Corina Hoffmann was beautiful. Her face, with its high cheekbones, Brigitte Bardot lips, her blonde, mussed-up, glossy hair. The long, thin arms emerging from the wide sleeves of the dressing gown, the tops of her breasts, so soft that they moved as she walked and when she breathed. And the white, white skin of her arms, face, breasts, legs—bloody hell, it was like snow glittering in sunlight, the way that can make a man snow-blind in just a few hours. Basically, I liked everything about Corina Hoffmann. Everything except her surname.

It looked like she was bored. She drank coffee. Talked on the phone. Leafed through a magazine, but ignored the newspapers. She disappeared into the bathroom, then came out again, still wearing the dressing gown. She put a record on, and danced along to it rather half-heartedly. Swing, it looked like. She had something to eat. Looked at the time. Almost six. She changed into a dress, fixed her hair and put a different record on. I opened the window and tried to hear, but there was too much traffic. So I picked up the binoculars again and tried to focus on the record-sleeve that she'd left on the table. It looked like there was a picture of the composer on the front. Antonio Lucio Vivaldi? Who knows? The point is that the woman Daniel Hoffmann came home to at quarter past six was a completely different one from the woman I had spent the whole day with.

They skirted around each other. Didn't touch each other. Didn't talk to each other. Like two electrons pushing away from each other because they're both negatively charged. But they ended up behind the same bedroom door.

I went to bed, but couldn't sleep.

What is it that makes us realise we're going to die? What is it that happens on the day when we acknowledge it isn't just a possibility, but an unavoidable fucking fact that our life will come to an end? Obviously everyone will have different reasons, but for me it was watching my father die. Seeing how banal and physical it was, like a fly hitting a windscreen. What's actually more interesting is: What is it—once we've reached that realisation— that makes us doubt again? Is it because we've gotten smarter? Like that philosopher—David Something-or-other—who wrote that just because something keeps happening, there's no guarantee that it's going to happen again. Without logical proof, we don't **know** that history is going to repeat itself. Or is it because we get older and more scared the closer it gets? Or is it something else entirely? As if one day we see something that we didn't know existed. Feel something that we didn't know we could feel. Hear a hollow sound when we bang on the wall, and realise that there might be another room behind it. And a hope is sparked, a terrible, draining hope that gnaws away at you and can't be ignored. A hope that there might be an escape route from death, a short cut to a place you didn't know about. That there is a point. That there is a narrative.

The next morning I got up at the same time as Daniel Hoffmann. It was still pitch-black when he left. He didn't know I was here. Didn't **want** to know, as he'd been careful to point out.

So I turned off the light, sat in the chair by the window and settled down to wait for Corina. I took out my papers again and looked through my letter project. The words were more incomprehensible than usual, and the few I did understand suddenly seemed irrelevant and dead. Why didn't I just throw the whole lot away? Because I'd spent so long composing those wretched sentences? I put it all down and studied the lack of activity on Oslo's deserted winter streets until she finally appeared.

The day passed much like the previous one. She went out for a while and I followed her. From following Maria I had learned the best way to do it without being noticed. Corina bought a scarf in a shop, drank coffee with someone who seemed to be a girl friend to judge from their body language, and then went home.

It was still only ten o'clock, and I made myself a cup of coffee. I watched her lying on the chaise longue in the middle of the room. She'd put a dress on, a different one. The fabric shifted around her body whenever she moved. A chaise longue is a strange piece of furniture, neither one thing nor the other. When she moved to find a more comfortable position it happened slowly, elaborately, consciously. As if she knew she was being watched. Knew that she was desired. She looked at the time, leafed through her magazine, the same as the day before. Then she tensed up, almost imperceptibly.

I couldn't hear the doorbell.

She stood up, went over to the door in that languid, soft, feline way, and opened it.

He was dark-haired, fairly thin, the same age as her.

He went in, shut the door behind him, hung up his coat and kicked off his shoes in a way that suggested this wasn't his first visit. Nor his second visit. There was no doubt about that. There had never been any doubt. So why had I doubted? Because I wanted to?

He hit her.

I was so shocked at first I thought I'd seen wrong. But then he did it again. Slapped her hard across the face with the flat of his hand. I could see from her mouth that she was screaming.

He took hold of her throat with one hand and pulled her dress off with the other.

There, under the chandelier, her naked skin was so white that it seemed to be a single surface, no contours, just an impenetrable whiteness, like snow in the flat light of an overcast or foggy day.

He took her on the chaise longue. Stood there at the foot of it with his trousers round his ankles while she lay on the pale, embroidered images of virginal, idealised European woodland landscapes. He was skinny. I could see his muscles moving under his ribcage. The muscles in his buttocks tensed and relaxed like a pump. He was shuddering and shaking, as if he were furious that he couldn't do anything . . . more. She lay there, legs open, passive, like a corpse. I wanted to look away, but couldn't. Seeing them like that reminded me of something. But I couldn't work out what.

Maybe I remembered what it was that night, once everything had calmed down. Either way, I dreamed about a picture I'd seen in a book when I was a boy. **Animal Kingdom 1: Mammals,** from the Deichman Library. It was a picture of the Serengeti savannah in Tanzania, somewhere like that. Three furious, scrawny, wound-up hyenas that had either managed to bring down their own prey, or had chased the lions away from theirs. Two of them, their buttocks tensed, had their jaws dug into the zebra's gaping stomach. The third was looking at the camera. Its head was smeared with blood and it was baring its jagged row of teeth. But it was the look in its eyes I remembered most. The look that those yellow eyes were directing into the camera and out of the page of the book. It was a warning. **This isn't yours, it's ours. Get lost. Or we'll kill you too.**

CHAPTER 4

When I stand behind you in the underground, I always wait until our carriage goes over a join in the rails before saying anything. Maybe it's a set of points where the track divides. Either way, somewhere deep underground where metal rattles and clatters against metal, a sound that reminds me of something, something to do with words, things falling into place, something to do with fate. The train lurches, and anyone who isn't a regular passenger momentarily loses their balance and has to reach out for support, anything that can help them stay upright. The change of tracks makes enough noise to drown out anything I might want to say. I whisper whatever I want to whisper. Right at that point when no one else can hear me. You wouldn't be able to hear me anyway. Only I can hear me.

What do I say?

I don't know. Just things that come into my head. Things. I don't know where they've come from, or if I really mean them. Well, maybe I do, there and then. Because you're beautiful, you too, as I stand there in the crowd right behind you, looking at just the bun in your hair and imagining the rest.

But I can't imagine that you're anything but dark-haired, because you are. You're not fair like Corina. Your lips aren't so full of blood that I want to bite them. There's no music in the sway of your back and the curve of your breasts. You've only been there until now because there hasn't been anyone else. You filled a vacuum that I never used to know existed.

You asked me back to yours for dinner that time, just after I'd got you out of trouble. I assumed it was as a thank-you. You wrote the invitation on a note and gave it to me. I said yes. I was going to write that down, but you smiled to let me know that you understood.

I never came.

Why not?

If I knew the answer to things like that . . .

I am me, and you are you? Maybe that was it.

Or was it even simpler? Like the fact that you're deaf and dumb and walk with a limp. I've got more than enough handicaps of my own. Like I said, I'm good for nothing apart from one thing. And what the hell would we have said to each other? You would doubtless have suggested that we write things down for each other, and I—as I've said—

am dyslexic. And if I haven't said it before, I'm saying it now.

And you can probably imagine, Maria, that a man doesn't get that fucking turned on by you laughing loudly and shrilly in that way deaf people do because he's managed to write "What lovely eyes you've got" with four separate spelling mistakes.

Whatever. I didn't go. That's all there was to it.

Daniel Hoffmann wanted to know why it was taking so long to get the job done.

I asked him if he agreed that I should take care not to leave any evidence that could be traced back to either of us before I got going. He agreed.

So I carried on watching the apartment.

Over the following days the young guy visited her every day at exactly the same time, three o'clock, right after it had got dark again. Came in, hung his coat up, hit her. It was the same every time. At first she would hold her arms up in front of her. I could see from her mouth and neck muscles that she was shouting at him, begging him to stop. But he didn't stop. Not until the tears were streaming down her cheeks. Then—and only then—would he pull her dress off. Every time a new dress. Then he would take her on the chaise longue. And it was obvious he had the upper hand. I suppose she must have been hopelessly in love with him. The way Maria was in love with her junkie boyfriend. Some women don't know what's best for them, they just leak love without demanding anything in return. It's almost as if the very lack of any reciprocation just makes them worse. I suppose they're hoping they'll be rewarded one day, poor things. Hopeful, hopeless infatuation. Someone ought to tell them that isn't how the world works.

But I don't think Corina was in love. She didn't seem interested in him like that. Okay, so she would caress him after they made love, and follow him to the door when he was about to leave, three-quarters of an hour after he arrived, and hold on to him in a slightly affected way, presumably whispering sweet nothings. But she seemed almost relieved once he had gone. And I like to think I know what love looks like. So why would she—the young wife of the city's leading purveyor of ecstasy—be willing to risk everything for a tawdry affair with a man who hit her?

It was the evening of the fourth day when it dawned on me. And my first thought after that was how strange it was that it had taken me so long to work it out. Her lover had something on her. Something he could take to Daniel Hoffmann if she didn't do as he wanted.

When I woke up on the fifth day I had made up my mind. I wanted to test the short cut to the place we didn't know about.

CHAPTER 5

It was snowing gently.

When the guy arrived at three o'clock he had brought something for her. Something in a little box. I couldn't see what it was, only that she lit up for a moment. She lit up the night darkness outside the large living-room window. She looked surprised. I was surprised myself. But I promised myself that the smile she had shown him, she'd let **me** have that. I just had to do this properly.

When he left, just after four—he stayed a bit longer than usual—I was standing ready in the shadows on the other side of the street.

I watched him disappear into the darkness and looked up. She was standing in front of the living-room window, like she was onstage, and held up her hand and studied something in it, I couldn't see what. Then she suddenly raised her eyes and stared at the shadows where I was standing. I knew she couldn't possibly have seen me, but still . . . That penetrating, searching look. Suddenly there was something scared, desperate, almost pleading in her face. "An awareness that fate can't be forced," as the book said, God knows which one. I squeezed the pistol in my coat pocket.

I waited until she had pulled back from the window, then stepped out of the shadows. I quickly crossed the street. On the pavement I could see his boot-prints in the fine dusting of fresh snow. I hurried after him.

I caught sight of his back as I went round the next corner.

Obviously I had thought through a number of possibilities.

He might have a car parked somewhere. In which case it would probably be somewhere in one of the back streets in Frogner. Deserted, poorly lit. Perfect. Or he might be going somewhere—a bar, a restaurant. In that case I could wait. I had all the time in the world. I **liked** waiting. I liked the time between making the decision and carrying it out. They were the only minutes, hours, days of my admittedly short life when I **was** someone. I was someone's destiny.

He might be going to take a bus or taxi. The advantage of that would be that we would end up a bit further away from Corina.

He was heading towards the underground station by the National Theatre.

There was hardly anyone about, so I moved closer.

He went down onto one of the westbound platforms. So he was from the west side of the city. Not somewhere I'd spent much time. Too much money, too little use for it, as my dad used to say. I've no idea what he meant by that.

It wasn't the line that Maria usually took, although they shared the track for the first few stations.

I sat in the seat behind him. We were in the tunnel, but there was no longer any difference between that and the night outside. I knew that we would soon reach the place. There would be a rattling of metal and the train would do that little lurch.

I toyed with the idea of putting the mouth of the pistol against the back of the seat and pulling the trigger as we passed that point.

And as we did that—passed it—I realised for the first time what it reminded me of. Metal against metal. A feeling of order, of things falling into place. Of destiny. It was the sound of my work, of the movable parts of a weapon—pin and hammer, bolt and recoil.

We were the only passengers who got off at Vinderen. I followed him. The snow crunched. I took care to match my steps to his, so he couldn't hear me. Detached villas on either side of us, but we were still so alone that we might as well have been on the moon.

I walked right up to him, and, as he half-turned, perhaps to see if it was one of his neighbours, I shot him in the base of the spine. He collapsed beside a fence and I turned him over with my foot. He stared at me with glassy eyes and for a moment I thought he was already dead. But then he moved his lips.

I could have shot him through the heart, in the neck or head. Why had I shot him in the back first? Was there something I wanted to ask him? Maybe, but I'd forgotten what now. Or it didn't feel important. He didn't look anything special close up. I shot him in the face. A hyena with a bloodstained snout.

I noticed a boy's head sticking up over the fence. He had lumps of snow on his mittens and hat. Maybe he'd been trying to make a snowman. It's not easy when the snow's so powdery. Everything keeps falling apart, crumbling between your fingers.

"Is he dead?" the boy asked, looking down at the corpse. Maybe it seems odd to call someone a corpse just a few seconds after the person in question has died, but that's the way I've always looked at it.

"Was he your dad?" I asked.

The boy shook his head.

I don't know why I thought that. Why I got the idea that just because the boy seemed so calm it must have been his father lying there dead. Well, I do know, actually. That's how I would have reacted.

"He lives there," the boy said, pointing with one mitten as he sucked at the snow on the other, not taking his eyes off the dead body.

"I won't come back and get you," I said. "But forget what I look like. Okay?"

"Okay." His cheeks were tensing and relaxing around the snow-covered mitten, like a baby sucking a nipple.

I turned and walked back the same way I had come. I wiped the handle of the pistol and dropped it in one of the drains on which the thin snow hadn't managed to settle. It would be found, but by the police rather than some careless kids. I never travelled by underground, bus or taxi after I'd fixed someone, that was forbidden. Normal, brisk walking, and if you saw a police car heading your way, you turned round and walked towards the scene of the crime. I had almost got as far as Majorstua before I heard any sirens.

CHAPTER 6

It was just a week or so ago. As usual I was waiting, hidden by the rubbish bins in the car park behind the supermarket after closing time. I heard the soft click as a door opened and then slammed shut again. It was easy to recognise Maria's footsteps from her limp. I waited a bit longer, then set off in the same direction. The way I see it, I'm not **following** her. Obviously she's the one who decides where we go, and that day we weren't going straight to the underground. We went via a florist's, then up to the cemetery by Aker Church. There was no one else there, and I waited outside so she wouldn't see me. When she came out again she no longer had the bouquet of yellow flowers. She carried on towards Kirkeveien, in the direction of the station, while I went into the cemetery. I found the flowers on a fresh but already frozen grave. The headstone was nice and shiny. A familiar, French-sounding name. There he was, her junkie. I hadn't realised he was dead. Evidently not many other people had either. There was no date of death, just a month, October, and the year. I thought they always guessed at a date if they weren't sure. So it didn't look so lonely. Less lonely, lying here among the crowd in a snow-covered cemetery.

Now, as I walked home, I thought about the fact that I could stop following her. She was safe. I hoped she felt that she was safe. I hoped that he, her junkie, had stood behind her on the train and whispered: "I won't come back and get you. But forget what I look like." Yes, that's what I hoped. I'm not going to follow you any more, Maria. Your life starts now.

I stopped by the phone box on Bogstadveien.

My life started then as well, with that phone call. I needed to be released from Daniel Hoffmann. That was the start. The rest was more uncertain.

"Fixed," I said.

"Good," he said.

"Not her, sir. Him."

"Sorry?"

"I fixed the so-called lover." On the phone we always say "fixed." As a precaution in case we're overheard or being bugged. "You won't see him again, sir. And they weren't really lovers. He was forcing her. I'm convinced she didn't love him, sir."

I had spoken quickly, more quickly than I usually do, and a long pause followed. I could hear

Daniel Hoffmann breathing heavily through his nose. Snorting, really.

"You . . . you killed Benjamin?"

I already knew I should never have called.

"You . . . you killed my only . . . son?"

My brain registered and interpreted the sound waves, translated them into words which it then began to analyse. Son. Was that possible? A thought began to form. The way the lover had kicked his shoes off. As if he'd been there many times before. As if he used to live there.

I hung up.

Corina Hoffmann stared at me in horror. She was wearing a different dress and her hair wasn't yet dry. It was quarter past five and—as on previous occasions—she had showered off all traces of the dead man before her husband came home.

I had just told her that I had been ordered to kill her.

She tried to slam the door shut, but I was too fast.

I got my foot inside and forced the door open. She stumbled backwards, into the light of the living room. She grabbed at the long chair. Like an actress onstage, making use of the props.

"I'm begging you . . ." she began, holding one arm out in front of her. I saw something sparkle. A big ring with a stone in it. I hadn't seen it before.

I took a step closer.

She started screaming loudly. Grabbed a table lamp and threw herself at me. I was so surprised by the attack that I only just managed to duck and avoid her wild swing. The force and momentum made her lose her balance and I caught hold of her. I felt her damp skin against the palms of my hands, and the heavy smell. I wondered what she had used in the shower. Unless it was her own smell? I held her tight, feeling her rapid breathing. Dear God, I wanted to take her, there and then. But no, I wasn't like him. I wasn't like them.

"I'm not here to kill you, Corina," I whispered into her hair. I inhaled her. It was like smoking opium—I felt myself going numb at the same time as all my senses quivered. "Daniel knows you had a lover. Benjamin. He's dead now."

"Is . . . is Benjamin dead?"

"Yes. And if you're here when Daniel gets home, he'll kill you too. You have to come with me, Corina."

She blinked at me in confusion. "Where to?"

It was a surprising question. I'd been expecting "Why?", "Who are you?" or "You're lying!" But maybe she instinctively realised that I was telling the truth, that it was urgent, maybe that was why she got straight to the point. Unless she was just so confused and resigned that she blurted out the first thing that came into her head.

"To the room beyond the room," I said.

CHAPTER 7

She was sitting curled up in the only arm-chair in my flat, staring at me.

She was even more beautiful like that: frightened, alone, vulnerable. Dependent.

I had—somewhat unnecessarily—explained that my flat wasn't much to boast about, basically just a simple bachelor pad with a living room and an alcove for the bed. Clean and tidy, but no place for a woman like her. But it had one big advantage: no one knew where it was. To be more precise: no one—and by that I do literally mean **no one**—knew where I lived.

"Why not?" she asked, clasping the cup of coffee I'd given her.

She'd asked for tea, but I'd told her she'd have to wait till morning, and that I'd get some as soon as the shops opened. That I knew she liked tea in the morning. That I'd watched her drinking tea every morning for the past five days.

"It's best if no one knows your address when you're in my line of work," I replied.

"But now I know."

"Yes."

We drank our coffee in silence.

"Does that mean you don't have any friends or relations?" she asked.

"I have a mother."

"Who doesn't know . . . ?"

"No."

"And obviously she doesn't know about your job either."

"No."

"What have you told her you do?"

"Fixer."

"Odd jobs?"

I stared at Corina Hoffmann. Was she really interested, or just talking for the sake of it?

"Yes."

"Right." A shiver ran through her and she folded her arms over her chest. I'd turned the oven on full, but with the single-glazed windows and temperatures down at minus twenty for over a week, the cold had got the upper hand. I fiddled with my cup.

"What do you want to do, Olav?"

I got up from the kitchen chair. "See if I can find you a blanket."

"I mean, what are **we** going to do?"

She was okay. You know someone's okay if they can ignore things they can't do anything about and move on. Wish I was like that.

"He's going to come after me, Olav. After us. We can't hide here for ever. And that's how long he'll go on looking. Believe me, I know him. He'd rather die than live with this shame."

I didn't ask the obvious question: So why did you take his son as your lover?

Instead I asked a less obvious one.

"Because of the shame? Not because he loves you?"

She shook her head. "It's complicated."

"We've got plenty of time," I said. "And as you can see, I haven't got a television."

She laughed. I still hadn't fetched that blanket. Or asked the question that for some reason I was desperate to ask: Did you love him? The son?

"Olav?"

"Yes?"

She lowered her voice. "Why are you doing this?"

I took a deep breath. I had prepared an answer to this question. Several answers, actually, in case I felt that the first one didn't work. At least, I thought I had prepared some answers. But at that moment they all vanished.

"It's wrong," I said.

"What's wrong?"

"What he's doing. Trying to have his own wife killed."

"And what would you have done if your wife was seeing another man in your own home?"

She had me there.

"I think you've got a good heart, Olav."

"Good hearts come cheap these days."

"No, that's not true. Good hearts are unusual. And always in demand. **You're** unusual, Olav."

"I'm not sure that's true."

She yawned and stretched. Lithe as a pussycat. They have really flexible shoulders, so wherever they can get their heads in, they can also squeeze their whole body. Practical for hunting. Practical for flight.

"If you've got that blanket, I think I might get some sleep now," she said. "There's been a bit too much excitement today."

"I'll change the bed, then you can have that," I said. "The sofa and I are old friends."

"Really?" she smiled, winking one of her big blue eyes. "Does that mean I'm not the first person to spend the night here?"

"No, you are. But sometimes I fall asleep reading on the sofa."

"What do you read?"

"Nothing special. Books."

"Books?" She tilted her head to one side and smiled mischievously, as if she'd caught me out. "But I can see only one book here."

"The library. Books take up space. Besides, I'm trying to cut down."

She picked up the book that was on the table. "**Les Misérables?** What's this one about, then?"

"Lots of things."

She raised an eyebrow.

"Mostly about a man who gets forgiveness for his sins," I said. "He spends the rest of his life making up for his past by being a good man."

"Hmm." She weighed the book in her hands. "It feels a bit heavy. Is there any romance in it?"

"Yes."

She put it down. "You didn't say what we're going to do, Olav."

"What we have to do," I said, "is fix Daniel Hoffmann before he fixes us."

The sentence had sounded stupid when I formulated it inside my head. And just as stupid when I said it out loud.

CHAPTER 8

I went to the hotel early the next morning. Both of the rooms that faced Hoffmann's apartment were already taken. I went and stood outside in the morning darkness, hidden behind a parked van, and looked up at his living room. Waiting. Squeezing the pistol in my coat pocket. This was the time he normally left home to go to work. But of course things weren't normal. The lights were on, but it was impossible to see if there was anyone up there. I presumed that Hoffmann realised I wouldn't have taken off with Corina and now be holed up in a hotel in Copenhagen or Amsterdam, say. To begin with, that wasn't my style, and anyway, I didn't have the money, and Hoffmann knew that. I'd had to ask for an advance to cover my expenses for this job. He'd asked why I was so broke, seeing as he'd only just paid me for two jobs. I said something about bad habits.

If Hoffmann was assuming that I was still in the city, then he would also assume that I'd try to get him before he got me. We knew each other fairly well by now. But it's one thing to think you know something about someone, and another to know for certain, and I've been wrong before. Maybe he was on his own up there. And if that was the case, I'd never get a better opportunity than when he emerged from the building. I'd just have to wait until the lock clicked shut behind him so he couldn't get back inside, run across the street, two shots to the torso from five metres, then two in the head from close range.

That was a lot to hope for.

The door opened. It was him.

And Brynhildsen and Pine. Brynhildsen with the toupee that looked like it was made from dog hair and the pencil-thin moustache that looked like a croquet hoop. Pine in the caramel-brown leather jacket he wore all year round, summer and winter alike. With his little hat, the cigarette tucked behind his ear, and a mouth that just wouldn't stop. Random words drifted across the street. "Fucking cold" and "that bastard."

Hoffmann stopped inside the doorway while his two attack dogs went out onto the pavement and looked up and down the street with their hands deep in their jacket pockets.

Then they waved at Hoffmann and began to walk towards the car.

I hunched my shoulders and headed in the opposite direction. Fine. It was, as I said, a lot to hope for. And now at least I knew that he had worked out how I was thinking of solving this. With him dying rather than me.

Either way, it meant I had to go back to Plan A.

The reason I had started with Plan B was that there wasn't a single thing I liked about Plan A.

CHAPTER 9

I like watching films. Not as much as reading books, but a good film has something of the same function. It encourages you to look at things differently. But no film has managed to persuade me to take a different view of the advantages of being in the majority and being more heavily armed. In a fight between one man and several others, in which both parties are pretty much prepared and armed, the one who's on his own will die. In a fight where one party has an automatic weapon, whoever has that weapon will win. This was the result of hard-won experience, and I wasn't about to pretend it wasn't true just so I wouldn't have to go and see the Fisherman. It was true. And that's why I went to see him.

The Fisherman, as I've already said, shares the heroin market in Oslo with Daniel Hoffmann. Not a big market, but because heroin was the main product, the customers were good at paying and the prices were high, the profits sky high. It all started with the Russian route—or the North Passage. When it was established by Hoffmann and the Russians in the early seventies, most of the heroin came from the Golden Triangle via Turkey and Yugoslavia, the so-called Balkan route. Pine had told me that he had been working as a pimp for Hoffmann, and that because ninety per cent of the prostitutes used heroin, getting paid with a fix was just as good as Norwegian kroner for most of them. So Hoffmann worked out that if he could get hold of cheap heroin, he'd be able to increase his takings from their sexual services accordingly.

The idea of getting hold of cheap gear didn't come from the south but the north. From the inhospitable little Arctic island of Svalbard which is shared between Norway and the Soviet Union, who each run coal mines on their respective sides of the island. Life there is hard and monotonous, and Hoffmann had heard Norwegian miners tell horror stories of how the Russians drowned their sorrows with vodka, heroin and Russian roulette. So Hoffmann went up and met the Russians, and came back home with an agreement. Raw opium was shipped from Afghanistan into the Soviet Union, where it was refined into heroin and then sent north to Archangel and Murmansk. It would have been impossible to get it across to Norway, seeing as the Communists guarded the border with Norway, a NATO country, so carefully—and vice versa. But on Svalbard, where the border was only guarded by polar bears and temperatures of minus forty degrees, there wasn't a problem.

Hoffmann's contact on the Norwegian side sent the goods with the daily domestic flight to Tromsø, where they never checked so much as a single suitcase, even if everyone knew the miners were bringing in litre upon litre of cheap, tax-free spirits. It was as if even the authorities thought they deserved that much of a bonus. Obviously they were the ones who claimed in hindsight that it was naive to think that so much heroin could be brought in and shipped on to Oslo by plane, railway and road without anyone knowing about it. And that a few envelopes must have ended up in the hands of public officials.

But according to Hoffmann not a single krone was paid. It simply wasn't necessary. The police had no idea what was going on. Not until an abandoned snow-scooter was found on the Norwegian side of the island, outside Longyearbyen.

The human remains left by the polar bears turned out to be Russian, and the petrol tank contained plastic bags holding a total of four kilos of pure heroin.

The operation was put on hold while the police and officials swarmed around the area like angry bees. A heroin panic broke out in Oslo. But greed is like meltwater: when one channel gets blocked it simply finds a new one. The Fisherman— who was many things, but first and foremost a businessman—put it like this: demand that isn't being met demands to be met. He was a jovial, fat man with a walrus moustache who made you think of Santa Claus, until it suited him to slash you with a Stanley knife. He'd spent a few years smuggling Russian vodka that was shipped out on Soviet fishing boats, transferred to Norwegian fishing boats in the Barents Sea, then unloaded at an abandoned fishing station that the Fisherman not only ran, but owned, lock, stock and barrel. There the bottles were loaded into fish crates and driven down to the capital in fish vans. There was fish in them as well. In Oslo the bottles were stored in the cellar of the Fisherman's shop, which was no fake front but a fishmonger's that had been in the Fisherman's family for three generations without ever being particularly profitable, but without going under either.

And when the Russians wondered if he could imagine swapping the vodka for heroin, the Fisherman did some calculations, looked at the legal penalties, looked at the risk of getting caught, then went for it. So, when Daniel Hoffmann started up his Svalbard trade again, he realised that he had competition. And he didn't like that at all.

And that was where I came into the picture.

By that time—as I think I've already made clear—I had a more-or-less failed criminal career behind me. I'd done time for bank robbery, worked for and got fired by Hoffmann as an assistant pimp to Pine, and was on the lookout for something vaguely useful to do. Hoffmann contacted me again because he'd heard from reliable sources that I had fixed a smuggler who was found in the harbour at Halden with his head only partially intact. A very professional contract killing, Hoffmann declared. And seeing as I had no better reputation at my disposal, I didn't deny it.

The first job was a man from Bergen who worked as a dealer for Hoffmann, but had stolen some of the goods, denied it, and had gone to work for the Fisherman instead. He was easy to track down: people from the west talk louder than other Norwegians, and his rolling Bergen **r**'s ripped through the air down by the central station where he was dealing. I let him see my pistol, and that put an abrupt halt to those rolling **r**'s. They say it's easier to kill the second time, and I suppose that's true. I took the guy down to the container port and shot him twice in the head to make it look like the Halden fix. Seeing as the police already had a suspect for the Halden case, they were on the wrong track from day one, and never came close to giving me any grief. And Hoffmann got confirmation of his conviction that I was fixer number one, and gave me another job.

This one was a young guy who'd called Hoffmann and said he'd rather deal for him than for the Fisherman. He wanted them to meet somewhere discreet so they could discuss the details without the Fisherman finding out. Said he couldn't stand the stink of the fishmonger's any more. He should probably have worked a bit harder on his cover story. Hoffmann got hold of me and said he thought the Fisherman had told the guy to fix him.

The following evening I was waiting for him at the top of the park at Sankt Hanshaugen. There's a good view from up there. People say it was once used for sacrifices, and that it's haunted. My mum told me printers used to boil ink there. All I know is that it's where the city's rubbish used to be burned. The forecast said it was going to be minus twelve degrees that evening, so I knew we'd be alone. At nine o'clock a man came walking up the long path to the tower. In spite of the cold his forehead was wet with sweat by the time he reached the top.

"You're early," I said.

"Who are you?" he asked, mopping his brow with his scarf. "And where's Hoffmann?"

We both reached for our pistols at the same time, but I was faster. I hit him in the chest and in the arm just above the elbow. He dropped his gun and fell backwards. Lay there in the snow blinking up at me.

I put the pistol to his chest. "How much did he pay?"

"Tw . . . twenty thousand."

"Do you think that's enough for killing someone?"

He opened and closed his mouth.

"I'm going to kill you anyway, so there's no need to come up with a smart answer."

"We've got four kids and we live in a two-room flat," he said.

"Hope he paid in advance," I said, and fired.

He groaned, but lay there blinking. I stared at the two holes in the front of his jacket. Then I tore the buttons open.

He was wearing chain mail. Not a bulletproof vest, but fucking chain mail, the sort the Vikings used to wear. Well, they did in the illustrations of Snorri's **Sagas of the Kings** that I read so many times as a boy that in the end the library refused to let me take it out any more. Iron. It was hardly surprising the climb up the hill had made him sweat.

"What the fuck's this?"

"My wife made it," he said. "For the play. About St. Olav."

I ran my fingers over the loops of metal, all hooked together. How many thousands of them could there be? Twenty? Forty?

"She won't let me go out without it," he said.

Chain mail, made for a play about the murder of a holy king.

I put the pistol against his forehead and fired. The third one. It should have been easier.

His wallet contained fifty kroner, a photograph of his wife and kids, and an ID card with his name and address.

Those fixes were two of the three reasons why I wanted to stay out of the Fisherman's way.

I went to his shop early the next day.

Eilertsen & Son Fishmonger's was located on Youngstorget, just a stone's throw from the central police station at 19 Møllergata. Word is that when the Fisherman still sold smuggled vodka, the police were among his best customers.

Huddled against the piercing, icy wind, I crossed the sea of cobbles.

The shop had only just opened when I stepped inside, but there were already plenty of customers.

Sometimes the Fisherman himself served in the shop, but not that day. The women behind the counter went on serving their customers, but a young man—I could tell from the look he gave me that he had other duties apart from just cutting, weighing and packing fish—vanished through a swing door.

Shortly afterwards the boss came in. The Fisherman. Dressed in white from top to toe. With an apron and cap. He even had white wood-soled sandals. Like some fucking lifeguard. He walked round the counter and came up to me. He wiped his fingers on the apron, which bulged over his stomach. Then nodded towards the door that was still swinging back and forth on its hinges. Each time there was a gap I could see a skinny, familiar figure. The one they called Klein. I don't know if it was the German sense of the word, small. Or the Norwegian, sick. Unless it really was his name. Maybe all three. Every time the door swung open, my eyes met his, dead, pitch black. I also got a glimpse of the sawn-off shotgun hanging down by his foot.

"Keep your hands out of your pockets," the Fisherman said quietly with his broad Santa Claus grin. "Then you might make it out of here alive."

I nodded.

"We're busy selling fish for Christmas, lad, so say what you came to say, then get the hell out of here."

"I can help you get rid of the competition."

"You?"

"Yes. Me."

"I didn't think you were the treacherous type, lad."

The fact that he called me lad instead of my name may have been because he didn't know it, or didn't want to show me any respect by using it, or else saw no reason to let me know how much— if anything—he knew about me. I guessed the last of the three.

"Can we talk in the back room?" I asked.

"Here will do fine, no one will overhear us."

"I shot Hoffmann's son."

The Fisherman screwed up one eye while the other stared at me. For a long time. Customers called out "Happy Christmas!" and let gusts of cold air into the warm, steamy shop as they headed out through the door.

"Let's go into the back," the Fisherman said.

Three men fixed. You have to be a bloody cold businessman not to bear a grudge against someone who has fixed three of your people. I just had to hope that my offer was good enough, and that the Fisherman was as cold as I thought he was. Like hell he didn't know my name.

I sat down at a worn wooden table. On the floor were sturdy polystyrene boxes full of ice, frozen fish and—if Hoffmann was right about the logistics—heroin. The room couldn't have been much more than five or six degrees. Klein didn't sit down, and while I was talking it was like he wasn't consciously thinking about the vicious shotgun he was holding, but the whole time its barrel was aimed at nothing but me. I ran through recent events without lying, but also without going into unnecessary detail.

When I was done the Fisherman went on staring with that fucking Cyclops eye of his.

"So you shot his son instead of his wife?"

"I didn't know it was his son."

"What do you think, Klein?"

Klein shrugged his shoulders. "It said in the papers that a guy had been shot in Vinderen yesterday."

"So I saw. Maybe Hoffmann and his fixer here have used what it said in the papers to cook up a story they were sure we'd believe."

"Call the police and ask what his name was," I said.

"We will," the Fisherman said. "Once you've explained why you spared Hoffmann's wife and are now keeping her hidden."

"That's my business," I said.

"If you're planning on getting out of here alive, you'd better start talking. Fast."

"Hoffmann used to hit her," I said.

"Which one?"

"Both of them," I lied.

"So? The fact that someone gets hit by someone stronger doesn't mean they don't deserve it."

"Specially not a whore like that," Klein said.

The Fisherman laughed. "Look at those eyes, Klein. The lad would like to kill you! I think he might just be in love."

"No problem," Klein said. "I'd like to kill him too. He was the one who took out Mao."

I had no idea which one of the three of the Fisherman's men was Mao. But it had said "Mauritz" on the driving licence of the guy in Sankt Hanshaugen, so maybe it was him.

"The Christmas fish is waiting," I said. "So what's it to be?"

The Fisherman tugged the end of his walrus moustache. I wondered if he ever managed to wash out the smell of fish. Then he stood up.

"'What loneliness is more lonely than distrust?' Do you know what that means, lad?"

I shook my head.

"No. That's what the guy from Bergen said when

he came over to us. That you were too simple for
Hoffmann to use as a dealer. He said you couldn't
put two and two together."

Klein laughed. I didn't respond.

"That's T. S. Eliot, boys," the Fisherman sighed.
"The loneliness of a suspicious man. Believe me, all
leaders end up suffering that loneliness sooner or
later. And plenty of husbands will feel it at least once
in their lives. But most fathers manage to escape it.
Hoffmann has had a taste of all three versions. His
fixer, his wife and his son. Almost enough to make
you feel sorry for him." He went over to the swing
door. Looked through the round window into the
shop. "So what do you need?"

"Two of your best men."

"You make it sound like we've got an army at our
disposal here, lad."

"Hoffmann's going to be expecting it."

"Really? Doesn't he think he's the one hunting
you now?"

"He knows me."

The Fisherman looked like he was trying to pull
his moustache off. "You can have Klein and the
Dane."

"How about the Dane and—"

"Klein and the Dane."

I nodded.

The Fisherman led me out into the shop. I walked
over to the door and wiped the condensation from
the inside of the glass.

Blood on Snow

There was a figure standing over by Operapassasjen. He hadn't been there when I arrived. There could be hundreds of reasons why a man would be waiting out there in the snow.

"Have you got a telephone number where— ?"

"No," I said. "I'll let you know when I need them. Is there a back door?"

On my way home through the back streets I reflected that it hadn't been a bad exchange. I had two men, I was still alive, and I'd learned something new. That T. S. Eliot had written that line about loneliness. I always thought it was that woman, whatever her name was? George Eliot? "Hurt? He'll never be hurt—he's made to hurt other people." Not that I believe poets. No more than I believe in ghosts, anyway.

CHAPTER 10

Corina prepared a simple meal with the
food I'd bought.

"Nice," I said when I'd finished, wiping my
mouth and pouring more water into our glasses.

"How did you end up here?" she asked.

"What do you mean, end up?"

"I mean . . . why do you do this? Why don't you
do whatever your father did, for instance? I pre-
sume he didn't—"

"He's dead," I said, draining my glass in one go.
The food had been a bit too salty.

"Oh. I'm sorry to hear that, Olav."

"Don't be. No one else is."

Corina laughed. "You're funny."

She was the first person ever to say that about me.

"Put a record on, then."

I put the Jim Reeves record on.

"You've got old-fashioned taste," she said.

"I haven't got many records."

"I don't suppose you dance either?"

I shook my head.

"And you haven't got any beer in the fridge?"

"Do you want beer?"

She looked at me with a wry smile, as if I'd said something funny again.

"Shall we sit on the sofa, Olav?"

She cleared the table while I made coffee. I thought that was quite nice. Then we sat down on the sofa. Jim Reeves was singing that he loves you because you understand him. It had got a bit milder during the course of the day, and outside the window big fat flakes of snow were drifting past.

I looked at her. Part of me was so tense it wanted to sit on the chair instead. A different part just wanted to put my arm round her narrow waist and pull her to me. Kiss her red lips. Stroke her glossy hair. Squeeze her a bit tighter, so hard that I feel the air being squeezed out of her, hear her gasp for breath, her breasts and stomach pushing out towards me. I was feeling light-headed.

Then the needle slid across to the middle of the record, lifted up and swung back as the vinyl slowly stopped turning.

I swallowed hard. Felt like lifting my hand. Putting it on the skin between her shoulder and neck. But it was shaking. Not just my hand, but the whole of me, like I'd got flu or something.

"Listen, Olav . . ." Corina leaned over towards me. I couldn't work out if the intense scent was mostly perfume or mostly her. I had to open my mouth to get more air. She picked up the book from the coffee table in front of me. "Would you mind reading out loud to me? The bit about love . . ."

"I would . . ." I began.

"Go on then," she said, curling her legs beneath her on the sofa. She put a hand on my arm. "I **love** love."

"But I can't."

"Of course you can!" she laughed, putting the open book in my lap. "Don't be embarrassed, Olav, read! It's only me. . . ."

"I suffer from word-blindness."

My blunt statement brought her up short and she blinked at me as if I'd hit her. Hell, I'd even surprised myself.

"Sorry, Olav, but . . . you said . . . I thought . . ." She stopped, and silence descended. I wished the record had still been playing. I closed my eyes.

"I read," I said.

"You read?"

"Yes."

"But how can you if you can't . . . see the words?"

"I see them. But sometimes I see them wrong. And then I have to look at them again." I opened my eyes. Her hand was still on my arm.

"But, how . . . how do you know you've seen them wrong?"

"Mainly because the letters don't form words that make any sense. But now and then I just see a different word and don't realise my mistake until much later. Sometimes the story I get into my head is completely different. So I sort of end up getting two stories for the price of one."

She laughed. A loud, bubbly laugh. Her eyes twinkled in the semi-darkness. I laughed too. It wasn't the first time I had told someone I was dyslexic. But it was the first time anyone had continued to ask questions. And the first time I had tried to explain it to someone who wasn't my mum or a teacher. Her hand slid off my arm. Sort of unnoticed. I'd been waiting for it. She was slipping away from me. But her hand slid into mine instead. And squeezed it. "You really **are** funny, Olav. And kind."

Along the bottom of the window the snow had started to settle. The snow crystals hooked onto each other. Like the links in a piece of chain mail.

"So tell me, then," she said. "Tell me about the love story in the book."

"Okay," I said, and looked down at the book on my lap. It was open at the page where Jean Valjean forces himself on the ruined, doomed prostitute. I changed my mind. And told her instead about Cosette and Marius. And about Éponine, the young girl who was raised into a life of crime, and was hopelessly in love with Marius, and who ends up sacrificing her life for love. Other people's love. I told the story again, this time leaving out none of the details.

"Oh, how wonderful!" Corina exclaimed when I had finished.

"Yes," I said. "Éponine is . . ."

". . . that Cosette and Marius had each other in the end."

I nodded.

Corina squeezed my hand. She hadn't let go of it once. "Tell me about the Fisherman."

I shrugged my shoulders. "He's a businessman."

"Daniel says he's a murderer."

"That too."

"What's going to happen once Daniel's dead?"

"Then you won't have anyone to be afraid of. The Fisherman doesn't wish you any harm."

"I mean, will the Fisherman take over the whole thing?"

"I suppose so, he hasn't got any other competition. Unless you were thinking . . . ?" I did my best to give her a wry smile.

She laughed out loud and gave me a playful shove. Who would have guessed I was a comedian deep down?

"Why don't we just run away?" she asked. "You and me, we'd manage fine, the pair of us. I could make the food and you could . . ."

The rest of the sentence was left hanging in the air like a half-finished bridge.

"I'd be happy to run away with you, Corina, but I haven't got a krone to my name."

"No? Daniel always says he pays his people well. Loyalty has to be bought, he says."

"I've spent it all."

"What on?" She nodded past me, meaning the flat, to suggest that neither it nor anything in it could have cost a fortune.

I shrugged again. "There was a widow with four kids. I was the one who made her a widow, so I . . . well, I had a moment of weakness and put what her husband had been promised to fix someone in an envelope. And that turned out to be everything I had. I never knew the Fisherman paid so well."

She gave me a sceptical look. I don't think it was one of Darwin's six universal facial expressions, but I knew what she meant. "You . . . you gave all your money to the widow of a man who was going to **kill** someone?"

Obviously I'd already worked out that what I'd done had been pretty stupid, even if I had felt I got something out of it in exchange. But when Corina put it like that, it sounded completely idiotic.

"So who was he going to kill?"

"Don't remember," I said.

She looked at me. "Olav, you know what?"

I didn't know what.

She put her hand against my cheek. "You really are very, very unusual."

Her eyes looked over my face, taking it in, bit by bit, as if she were consuming it. I know that's the moment when you're supposed to know, when you're supposed to read the other person's thoughts, realise. Maybe that's true. My being dyslexic might explain it. My mum used to say I was too pessimistic. Maybe that's true as well. Either way, I was pleasantly surprised when Corina Hoffmann leaned over and kissed me.

We made love. It's not out of modesty that I choose this romantic, chaste euphemism instead of a more direct, instrumental word. But because making love really was the most fitting description. Her mouth was close to my ear, her breath teasing me. I held her incredibly carefully, like one of the dried flowers I sometimes found in the pages of books from the library, so brittle and fragile that they dissolved under my fingers as soon as I touched them. I was scared she would disappear. At regular intervals I raised myself up on my arms to check that she really was still there, that it wasn't just a dream. I stroked her, lightly as a feather, and very gently, so as not to use her up. I held back before entering her. She looked at me in surprise—she had no way of knowing that I was waiting for the right moment. And then it came, the moment, the melting together, this thing that you might imagine to be trivial for a former pimp, but which was nonetheless so overwhelming that I felt my throat tighten. She let out a low, drawn-out groan as I pushed into her, incredibly slowly and carefully, as I whispered something tender and idiotic in her ear. I recognised her impatience, but I wanted it to be like this, wanted it to be something special. So I took her at a measured pace, and with hard-fought self-control. But her hips began to roll like sharp, quick waves beneath me, and her white skin shimmered in the darkness. It was like holding moonlight. Just as soft. Just as impossible.

"Stay with me, my love," the breath in my ear panted. "Stay with me, my love, my Olav."

I smoked a cigarette. She slept. It had stopped snowing. The wind which had been playing a mournful tune on the guttering had packed up its instruments. The only sound in the room was her even breathing. I listened and listened. Nothing.

It had been just like I had dreamed it would be. And hadn't believed it could be. I was so tired that I had to get some sleep. But so happy that I didn't want to. Because when I fell asleep, this world, this world that I had never much cared for until now, would cease to exist for a while. And, according to that Hume guy, the fact that I had until now woken up every morning in the same body, into the same world, where what had happened had actually happened, was no guarantee that the same thing would happen again tomorrow morning. For the first time in my life, closing my eyes felt like a gamble.

So I went on listening. Keeping watch over what I had. There were no sounds that shouldn't have been there. But I carried on listening anyway.

CHAPTER 11

My mother was so weak. That was why she had to put up with more than even the strongest person could have handled.

For instance, she could never say no to my bastard of a father. Which meant she had to put up with more beatings than someone banged up for sex offences. He was especially fond of throttling her. I'll never escape the sound of my mum bellowing like a cow in the bedroom each time my father let go long enough for her to catch her breath, so that he could start strangling her all over again. She was too weak to say no to drink, which meant she downed enough poison to fell an ox or an elephant, even though she was only small. And she was so weak when it came to me that she gave me everything I ever wanted, even when she really needed what she was giving me.

People always said I was like my mum.

Only when I was staring into my father's eyes for

the last time did I realise that I had him inside me as well. Like a virus, an illness in my blood.

As a rule he only came to us when he needed money. And as a rule he got what little we had. But he also realised that to maintain the fear factor—no matter whether he got a handout or not—he had to demonstrate what would happen the day she **didn't** pay up. My mother would blame black eyes and thick lips on stairs, doors and slippery bathroom floors. And, as the drinking took hold, it did actually happen that she fell or banged into walls entirely of her own accord.

My father said I was studying to become an idiot. I suspect he may have had the same trouble reading and writing as I did, the difference being that he had given up. While he had dropped out of school at the earliest opportunity and hardly even read a newspaper after that, I actually had liked school, weirdly enough. Apart from math. I didn't say much, and most people probably thought I was stupid. But the Norwegian teacher who marked my work said I had something, something behind all the spelling mistakes, something the others didn't have. And that was more than enough for me. But my father used to ask what I thought I was going to do with all that reading. If I thought I was better than he and the rest of the family. They'd managed fine, doing honest work. They never tried to put on airs by learning fancy words and getting lost in stories. When I was sixteen I asked why he didn't try doing a bit of honest work himself. He beat me black and blue. Said he was raising a kid, and that was enough work for one day.

When I was nineteen he came round one evening. He had been let out of Botsen prison the same day, after a year inside for killing a man. There hadn't been any witnesses, so the court had agreed with the defence that the injuries to the man's brain **could** have been caused when he tried to fight back and slipped on the ice.

He made some remark about my having grown. Slapped me jovially on the back. My mum had said I was working in a warehouse, was that right? Had I finally come to my senses?

I didn't answer, didn't say I was working part-time as well as going to college to save money so I could get a small flat when I started at university after my military service the following year.

He said it was good I had a job, because now I'd have to cough up.

I asked why.

Why? He was my father, victim of a miscarriage of justice who needed all the help his family could give him to get back on his feet.

I refused.

He stared at me in disbelief. And I could see he was wondering whether to hit me. That he was sizing me up. His little boy **had** grown up.

Then he let out a short laugh. And said if I didn't hand over my pathetic savings, he'd kill my mother.

And make it look like an accident. What did I think about that?

I didn't answer.

He said I had sixty seconds.

I said the money was in the bank, and he'd have to wait till they opened the next morning.

He tilted his head, as if that would help him work out whether I was lying.

I said I wasn't going to run, that he could have my bed, and I'd sleep in Mum's room.

"So you've taken over my place there as well, have you?" he sneered. "Don't you know that's illegal? Or doesn't it say that in your books?"

That evening Mum and Dad shared the last of her drink. They went into her room. I lay on the sofa and stuffed my ears with toilet paper. But it didn't block out her bellowing. Then a door slammed, and I heard him go into my room.

I waited until two o'clock before I got up, went into the bathroom and got the toilet brush. Then I went down to the cellar and unlocked our store cupboard. I'd been given a pair of skis when I was thirteen. By my mum. God knows what she had to go without to pay for those skis. But they were too small now, I'd grown out of them. I pulled the snow-guard off one of the poles and went back up. I crept into my room. My father was lying on his back, snoring. I stood with a foot on each side of the narrow bed-frame, put the point of the ski pole against his stomach. I didn't want to risk his chest, because the spike might hit his sternum or one of his ribs. I put one hand through the strap on the pole, put the other one on top, and made sure the pole was at the right angle so that it wouldn't bow or snap the bamboo shaft. I waited. I don't know why, it wasn't that I was scared. I wasn't. His breathing became more unsettled, soon he'd move and roll over. So I jumped up, bending my knees under me like a ski jumper. And landed with my full weight. His skin offered some resistance, but once the hole was made the pole thrust right through him. The bamboo stick dragged part of his T-shirt with it into his stomach, and the spike bored deep into the mattress.

His eyes were black with shock as he lay there staring up at me. I'd been quick to sit on his chest so that his arms were locked down by my knees. He opened his mouth to scream. I took aim and rammed the toilet brush into his mouth. He gurgled and wriggled, but he couldn't move. Sure I'd fucking grown.

I sat there, feeling the bamboo pole behind the small of my back, with his body struggling beneath me. And I thought to myself that I was riding my father. Now my father was my bitch.

I don't know how long I sat there before he stopped struggling and his body became limp enough for me to risk removing the toilet brush.

"Fucking moron," he groaned, his eyes closed. "You cut someone's throat with a knife, not . . ."

Blood on Snow

"That would have been too quick," I said.

He laughed, and coughed. Bubbles of blood at the corners of his mouth.

"Now, **that's** my boy."

That was the last thing he said. So he got the last word after all. Because I realised there and then that he was right, the bastard. I **was** his boy. It isn't true that I didn't know why I waited those extra seconds before sticking the pole into him. It was to prolong the magical moment when I, and I alone, had power over life and death.

That was the virus I had in my blood. His virus.

I carried the corpse down into the cellar and wrapped it up in the old, rotten canvas tent. My mum had bought that for me as well. She had got it into her head that we, her little family, would go on camping trips. Cook freshly caught trout beside a lake where the sun never set. I hope she got there with her drinking.

More than a week passed before the police came to ask if we'd seen my father after he was released. We said no. They said they'd make a note of it. Thanked us, and left. They didn't seem particularly bothered. By that time I had already hired a van and taken the mattress and bedclothes to the dump to be incinerated. And that night I had driven deep into the far reaches of Nittedal, to a lake where the sun never sets, but where I wouldn't be fishing for trout for a good long while.

I sat there on the shore looking out over the sparkling surface, thinking that this is what we leave behind, a few ripples in water, there for a while and then gone. As if they'd never been there. As if we had never been here.

That was the first time I fixed someone.

A few weeks later I got a letter from the university: "It is with great pleasure that we can confirm that you have been accepted to . . ." with a date and time for registration. I slowly tore it into pieces.

CHAPTER 12

I was woken by a kiss.

Before I realised it was a kiss, there was a moment of pure and utter panic.

Then it all came back, and the panic was replaced by something warm and soft that, in the absence of any better word, I can only call happiness.

She had rested her cheek on my chest and I looked down at her, and the way her hair was flowing over me.

"Olav?"

"Yes?"

"Can't we just stay here for ever?"

I couldn't think of anything I'd rather do. I pulled her closer to me. Held her. Counting the seconds. Those were seconds we had together, seconds no one could take away from us, seconds we consumed there and then. But—like I said— I can't count for very long. I put my lips to her hair.

"He'd find us here, Corina."

"Let's go far away, then."

"We have to deal with him first. We can't spend the rest of our lives looking over our shoulders."

She ran one finger down my nose and chin, as if there was a seam there. "You're right. But then we can go, can't we?"

"Yes."

"Promise?"

"Yes."

"Where to?"

"Wherever you want."

She ran her finger down my neck, over my throat and between my collarbones. "In that case, I want to go to Paris."

"Paris it is, then. Why there?"

"Because that's where Cosette and Marius were together."

I laughed, swung my feet down onto the floor and kissed her on the forehead.

"Don't get up," she said.

So I didn't get up.

At ten o'clock I was reading the paper and drinking a cup of coffee at the kitchen table. Corina was asleep.

The record-breaking cold was continuing. But the milder weather yesterday had made the roads like glass. A car had slid onto the wrong side of the Trondheim road. A family of three on their way up north for Christmas. And the police still had no leads on the murder in Vinderen.

Blood on Snow

· · ·

At eleven o'clock I was standing in a department store. It was full of people looking for Christmas presents. I stood by the window, pretending to look at a dinner service while I watched the building on the other side of the road. Hoffmann's office. There were two men standing outside. Pine, and a guy I hadn't seen before. The new guy was stamping his feet, and the smoke from his cigarette was drifting right into Pine's face, who said something the other man didn't seem very interested in. He wore a huge bearskin hat and overcoat, but he still had his shoulders hunched up to his ears, while Pine looked relaxed in his dog-shit-coloured jacket and clown's hat. Pimps are used to standing outside. The new guy pulled his hat further down over his ears. But I think this was more because of Pine's verbal diarrhoea than the cold. Pine had taken the cigarette from behind his ear and was showing it to the other guy. Presumably he was telling the same old story, about how he'd had that cigarette there since the day he stopped smoking. That it was his way of showing the tobacco who was in charge. I reckon he just wanted people to ask him why he had a cigarette tucked behind his ear, so he could then bore the shit out of them.

He was wearing too many clothes for me to be able to see if he had a gun, but Pine's jacket was lopsided. A seriously fat wallet, or a shooter. Too heavy for it to be that vicious knife he went round with. Presumably the same knife he had used the time he persuaded Maria to work for him. Showing her what the knife could do to her, to her boyfriend, if she didn't suck and fuck back the money he owed. I had seen the terror in Maria's wide-open eyes, staring at his mouth, trying desperately to lipread what Pine wanted as he rattled on. Like he was now. But the new guy was ignoring the pimp and looking up and down the street with a dark glare from beneath his bearskin hat. Calm, focused. Must have been hired in. From abroad, maybe. He looked professional.

I left the shop through the door onto the next street. Went into a phone box on Torggata. Held up a page of the newspaper that I'd torn out. Drew a heart on the steamed-up window of the phone box while I waited for the call to be picked up.

"Ris Church, parish office."

"Sorry to bother you, but I've got a wreath I want to deliver for the Hoffmann funeral the day after tomorrow."

"The undertakers can look after—"

"The problem is that I live outside the city and am going to be driving through the city late tomorrow evening, after closing time. I thought I might deliver the wreath directly to the church."

"We don't have any staff who—"

"But I was assuming that you'd be receiving the coffin tomorrow evening?"

"That would be the normal way of things, yes."

I waited, but nothing more followed.

"Perhaps you could check for me?"

A barely audible sigh. "One moment." The sound of paper rustling. "Yes, that's right."

"Then I'll call in to the church tomorrow evening. I'm sure the family will want to see him one last time, so I'll be able to pass on my condolences to them as well. They've probably arranged a time with you to be let down into the crypt. I could call the family directly, but I'm reluctant to bother them. . . ."

I waited, listening to the silence at the other end. I cleared my throat: ". . . at this tragic time for them, so close to Christmas."

"I can see that they've asked to come between eight and nine o'clock tomorrow evening."

"Thank you," I said. "But I'm afraid I can't make it then. It might be just as well if you don't mention to them that I was thinking of coming in person. I'll try to find another way of delivering the wreath."

"As you wish."

"Thanks for your help."

I walked to Youngstorget. There was no one standing in Operapassasjen today. If it had been Hoffmann's man there the day before, then he'd seen what he wanted to see.

The young guy refused to let me behind the

counter. Said the Fisherman was in a meeting. I could see shadows moving behind the glass in the swing door. Then one of the shadows stood up and went out the same way I had done, through the back door.

"You can go through," the young guy said.

"Sorry," the Fisherman said. "It's not just fish for Christmas that people are making a fuss about."

I must have screwed up my nose at the strong smell, because he started to laugh.

"Don't you like the smell of skate, lad?" He nodded towards the fish that had been partially filleted on the counter behind us. "Shipping dope in the same truck as a load of skate works perfectly, you know. The sniffer dogs don't stand a chance. Not many people do it, but I like making fish balls from skate. Try one." He nodded towards a bowl on the tiled wooden table between us. Pale grey fish balls floated in a cloudy liquid.

"So how are things going with that side of the business?" I asked, acting as if I hadn't heard his invitation.

"There's nothing wrong with demand, but the Russians are starting to get greedy. They'll be easier to deal with when they can no longer play me and Hoffmann off against each other."

"Hoffmann knows that you and I have been talking."

"He's not stupid."

"No. Which is why he's well guarded these days. We can't just go and take him out. We'll need to have a bit of imagination."

"Your problem," the Fisherman said.

"We need to get on the inside."

"Still your problem."

"The death was announced in the paper today. Hoffmann junior is being buried the day after tomorrow."

"And?"

"That's where we can take Hoffmann."

"The funeral. Nice." The Fisherman shook his head. "Too risky."

"Not the funeral. The evening before. In the crypt."

"Explain."

I explained. He shook his head. I went on. He shook his head even more. I held one hand up and carried on talking. He was still shaking his head, but now he was grinning. "Well! How on earth did you come up with that?"

"Someone I know was buried at the same church. And that's how it worked then."

"You know I should say no."

"But you're going to say yes."

"And if I don't?"

"I'll need money for three coffins," I said. "Kimen Funeral Directors have them ready-made. But you probably know that. . . ."

The Fisherman looked at me warily. Wiped his

fingers on his apron. Tugged at his moustache. Wiped his fingers on his apron.

"Have a fish ball, and I'll see what I've got in the till."

I sat there and looked at the fish balls swimming in what I would have guessed was semen if I didn't know better. Actually, when I came to think about it, I **didn't** know better.

I walked past Maria's supermarket on the way home. It occurred to me that I might as well buy food for dinner there. I went in and grabbed a basket. She was serving a customer with her back to me. I walked along the aisles and picked out fish fingers, potatoes and carrots. Four beers. They had an offer on King Haakon chocolates, ready-wrapped in Christmas paper. I put a box in the basket.

I walked towards Maria's checkout. There was no one else in the shop. I saw she had seen me. She was blushing. Damn. I suppose it wasn't so strange, the business about dinner that time was probably still a bit raw, she probably didn't invite many men back to hers like that.

I went up to her and said a quick hello. Then looked down at my basket as I concentrated on putting the food—the fish fingers, potatoes, carrots and beer—on the conveyor belt. I held the box of chocolates in my hand for a moment. Hesitating. The ring on Corina's finger. The one he, the son, had given her. Just like that. And here I was, thinking of turning up with a box of fucking chocolates as a Christmas present, wrapped up like it was Cleopatra's crown jewels.

"Was. That. It."

I looked at Maria in surprise. She had spoken. Who the hell knew she could do that? It sounded strange, obviously. But it was words. Words, as good as any others. She brushed her hair from her face. Freckles. Gentle eyes. A bit tired.

"Yes," I said, overemphasising the word. Stretching my mouth.

She smiled slightly.

"That . . . is . . . it," I said slowly, and rather too loudly.

She gestured questioningly towards the box of chocolates.

"For . . . you." I held it out. "Happy . . . Christmas."

She put a hand over her mouth. And behind the hand her face ran through a whole range of expressions. More than six. Surprise, confusion, joy, embarrassment, followed by raised brows (**why?**), lowered eyelids and a grateful smile. That's what happens when you can't talk—you end up with a very expressive face, and learn to perform a sort of pantomime that looks a bit exaggerated to anyone who's not used to it.

I handed her the box. Saw her freckled hand approach mine. What did she want? Was she thinking of taking my hand? I pulled it back. Gave her a quick nod and headed for the door. I could feel her eyes on my back. Damn. All I'd done was give her a box of chocolates, so what exactly did the woman want?

The flat was dark when I let myself in. On the bed I could make out Corina's shape.

So quiet and motionless that I almost found it odd. I walked slowly over to the bed and stood above her. She looked so peaceful. And so pale. A clock began to tick inside my head, ticking as if it were working something out. I leaned closer to her, until my face was right above her mouth. Something was missing. And the clock was ticking louder and louder.

"Corina," I whispered.

No reaction.

"Corina," I repeated, a bit louder, and heard something I had never heard before in my own voice, a faint note of helplessness.

She opened her eyes.

"Come here, teddy bear," she whispered, wrapping her arms around me and pulling me down onto the bed.

"Harder," she whispered. "I won't break, you know."

No, I thought, you won't break. We, **this,** won't break. Because this is what I've been waiting for;

this is what I've been practising for. Nothing but death can ruin this.

"Oh, Olav," she whispered. "Oh, Olav."

Her face was glowing, she was laughing, but her eyes were shiny with tears. Her breasts shone white beneath me, so white. And even if at that moment she was as close as you can ever be to another person, it was as if I was looking at her the way I had first seen her, from a distance, behind a window on the other side of the street. And I thought that you can't see a person more nakedly than that, when they don't know they're being watched, studied. She had never seen me like that. Maybe she never would. Then it struck me. I still had those sheets of paper, the letter, the one I had never quite finished. And if Corina found it, she might misunderstand. All the same, it was odd that my heart started to beat faster because of a little thing like that. The sheets of paper were under the cutlery tray in the kitchen drawer, and there was no reason for anyone to move that. But I made up my mind to get rid of them at the earliest opportunity.

"That's it, Olav, like that."

Something loosened inside me when I came, something that had been lying there shut away. I don't know what it was, but the pressure from my ejaculation shook it out and revealed it. I lay back, gasping for breath. I was a changed man, I just didn't know in what way.

She leaned over me and tickled my forehead.

"How do you feel, my king?"

I answered, but my throat was full of saliva.

"What?" she laughed.

I cleared my throat and repeated: "Starving."

She laughed even louder.

"And happy," I said.

Corina couldn't stand fish. She was allergic to it, always had been, something in her family.

The supermarkets were all shut now, but I said I could order a CP Special from Chinese Pizza.

"Chinese Pizza?"

"Chinese food and pizzas. Separately, I mean. I have dinner there almost every day."

I got dressed again and went down to the phone box on the corner. I had never had a telephone installed in the flat, didn't want one. I didn't want people to have a way to hear me, find me, talk to me.

From the phone box I could see up to my window on the fourth floor. And I could see Corina standing there, her head circled in light like some fucking halo. She was looking down at me. I waved. She waved back.

Then the coin fell with a metallic gulp.

"Chinese Pizza, how can I help you?"

"Hi, Lin, it's Olav. One CP Special, takeaway."

"No eat here, Mistel Olav?"

"Not today."

"Fifteen minute."

"Thanks. One more thing. Has anyone been in asking about me?"

"Ask about you? No."

"Great. Is there anyone sitting there that you've seen me eating with before? Anyone with a funny thin moustache that looks like it has been drawn on? Or in a brown leather jacket with a cigarette tucked behind his ear?"

"Let's see. Nooo . . ."

There were only about ten tables, so I believed him. Neither Brynhildsen nor Pine was waiting for me. They'd been there with me on more than one occasion, but presumably they didn't know just how much of a regular I was. Good.

I shoved open the heavy metal door of the phone box and peered up at the window. She was still standing there.

It took a quarter of an hour to walk to Chinese Pizza. The pizza was waiting in a red cardboard box the size of a camping table. CP Special. The best in Oslo. I was looking forward to seeing Corina's face when she tasted her first bite.

"See you latel, all-a-gatol," Lin called as usual as I headed out of the door, which swung shut behind me before I had time to reply with the crocodile rhyme.

I hurried away along the pavement and swung

round the corner. I was thinking about Corina. I must have been thinking about Corina **very** hard. At least that's the only excuse I have for the fact that I didn't see them, hear them, or even think the obvious thought: that if they had worked out that it was my regular haunt, then they'd also have worked out that it might have occurred to me that they might have worked it out, and that I therefore wouldn't go anywhere near it without a degree of caution. So they weren't waiting inside in the warmth and light, but outside in the frozen darkness of space, where I could have sworn that even molecules were having trouble moving.

I heard two steps crunch on the snow, but the bastard pizza slowed me down and I didn't have time to draw my pistol before I felt cold hard metal pressing against my ear.

"Where is she?"

It was Brynhildsen. His pencil-thin moustache moved when he spoke. He had a young guy with him who looked more scared than dangerous, and who might as well have had a "trainee" badge on his jacket, but he still did a thorough job of searching me. I guessed Hoffmann had the sense to get the young lad to help Brynhildsen without arming him. Maybe he had a knife or something hidden away. Pistols were confirmation gifts.

"Hoffmann says you can live if we can have his wife," Brynhildsen said.

That was a lie, but I'd have said the same thing

myself. I considered my options. The street was empty of traffic and people. Apart from the wrong people. And it was so quiet that I could hear the spring in the trigger mechanism complain gently as it stretched.

"Fine," Brynhildsen said. "We can find her without you, you know."

He was right, he wasn't bluffing.

"Okay," I said. "I only took her to have something to bargain with. I had no idea the guy was a Hoffmann."

"I don't know anything about that. We just want the wife."

"We'd better go and get her, then," I said.

CHAPTER 13

W e **have** to take the underground," I explained. "Look, she thinks I'm protecting her. And I am. Unless I can use her in a deal like this. So I told her that if I wasn't home in half an hour, something serious must have happened and she should take off. And it'll take at least three-quarters of an hour by car to get to my flat through the Christmas traffic."

Brynhildsen stared at me. "So call her and say you're going to be a bit late."

"I haven't got a phone."

"Really? So how come the pizza was waiting for you when you arrived, Johansen?"

I looked down at the big red cardboard box. Brynhildsen was no idiot. "Phone box."

Brynhildsen ran his finger and thumb over either side of his moustache, as if he were trying to stretch the hairs. Then looked up and down the street. Presumably estimating the traffic. And wondering what Hoffmann would say if she got away.

"CP Special." This from the young lad. He was grinning broadly as he nodded towards the box. "Best pizza in the city, eh?"

"Shut up," Brynhildsen said, now finished with his moustache-stroking, having made up his mind.

"We'll take the underground. And we'll call Pine from your phone box and get him to pick us up out there."

We walked the five minutes it took to get to the underground station by the National Theatre. Brynhildsen pulled the sleeve of his coat down to cover the pistol.

"You'll have to get your own ticket, **I'm** not paying for it," he said as we stood at the ticket booth.

"The one I got when I came in is valid for an hour," I lied.

"That's true," Brynhildsen said with a grin.

I could always hope for a ticket inspection, and that they'd take me to some nice, safe police station.

The underground was as crowded as I had hoped. Weary commuters, gum-chewing teenagers, men and women wrapped up against the cold, with Christmas presents sticking out of plastic bags. So we had to stand. We positioned ourselves in the middle of the carriage, each of us with a hand on the shiny steel pole. The doors closed and the passengers' breath began to build up on the windows again. The train pulled away.

"Hovseter. I wouldn't have had you down as living out west, Johansen."

"You shouldn't believe everything you believe, Brynhildsen."

"Really? You mean like the fact that I'd have thought you could get pizza out in Hovseter rather than having to come all the way into the city?"

"It's a CP Special," the young lad said respectfully, staring at the red box that was taking up a ridiculous amount of space in the overfull carriage. "You can't get—"

"Shut up. So you like cold pizza, Johansen?"

"We reheat it."

"**We?** You and Hoffmann's wife?" Brynhildsen laughed his one-snort laugh—it sounded like an axe falling. "You're right, Johansen. We really shouldn't believe everything we believe."

No, I thought. You, for instance, shouldn't believe that a guy like me would seriously believe that a man like Hoffmann was going to let him live. And, given that someone like me didn't believe that, you shouldn't believe that he wouldn't take desperate measures to change the state of play. Brynhildsen's eyebrows almost met at the top of his nose.

Obviously I couldn't read what was going on in there, but I'd guess the plan was to shoot Corina and me in my flat. Then put the pistol in my hand and make it look like I'd shot her, then myself. A suitor driven mad by love, the old classic. A better option than dumping us in a lake in a valley just outside Oslo. Because if Corina just disappeared, her husband would automatically be the main suspect, and there wasn't a lot about Hoffmann that would stand up to close scrutiny. Well, that's what I'd have done if I was Brynhildsen. But Brynhildsen wasn't me. Brynhildsen was a man with an inexperienced sidekick, a pistol hidden up one sleeve and the other hand loosely grasping a metal pole, but without the space to spread his legs far enough to keep his balance. That's just the way it is when you're a first-timer on this line. I counted down. I knew every jolt of the rails, every movement, every comma and full stop.

"Hold this," I said, pushing the pizza box into the chest of the young guy, who automatically took it.

"Hey!" Brynhildsen shouted over the sound of shrieking metal, and raising the hand holding the pistol at the very second we hit the points. I started moving as the lurching of the train made Brynhildsen fling out his pistol arm in reflex as he tried to keep his balance. I grabbed the pole with both hands and levered myself past it with full force. I was aiming for the point where his eyebrows almost joined up at the top of his nose. I've read that a human head weighs about four and a half kilos, which, at a speed of seventy kilometres an hour, gives the sort of force that would take someone better at math than me to work out. When I leaned back again, there was a fine spray of blood coming from Brynhildsen's broken nose, and his eyes were almost all whites, just a little bit of the irises visible under his eyelids, and he was holding his arms out stiffly from his sides, like a penguin. I could see Brynhildsen was out for the count, but to prevent any potential revival, I grabbed both his hands in mine, so that one of my hands was holding the pistol up his sleeve, making it look like we were doing some sort of folk dance, the two of us. Then I repeated the previous move, seeing as it had had such a successful outcome the first time. I pulled him hard towards me, lowered my head and smashed into his nose. I heard something break that probably wasn't supposed to break. I let go of him, but not his pistol, and he collapsed in a heap while the other people standing around us gasped and tried to move away.

I spun round and aimed the pistol at the apprentice, as a nasal, studiously disinterested voice over the loudspeaker announced "Majorstua."

"My stop," I said.

His eyes were wide open above the pizza box, his mouth gawping so much that in a perverse way it was almost flirtatious. Who knew, maybe in a few years' time he'd be after me with more experience, better armed. Mind you, years? These youngsters learned all they needed to in three or four months.

The train braked as it pulled into the station. I backed towards the door behind me. All of a sudden we had plenty of space—people were pressed up against the walls staring at us. A baby was babbling to its mother, but otherwise no one made a sound. The train stopped and the doors slid open. I took another step back and stopped in the doorway. If there was anyone behind me trying to get on, they very wisely chose a different door.

"Come on," I said.

The kid didn't react.

"Come on," I said, more emphatically.

He blinked, still not understanding.

"The pizza."

He took a step forward, listless as a sleepwalker, and handed me the red box. I stepped back onto the platform. I stood there, pointing the pistol straight at the youth to make sure he realised that this was **my** stop alone. I glanced at Brynhildsen. He was lying flat on the floor, but one shoulder was twitching slightly, like an electric charge in something that was fucked but not quite ready to die.

The doors slid shut.

The kid stared at me from behind the filthy, wintry, salt-streaked windows. The train set off towards Hovseter and environs.

"See you latel, all-a-gatol," I whispered, lowering the pistol.

I walked home quickly through the darkness, listening for police sirens. As soon as I heard them, I put the pizza box on the steps of a closed bookshop and began to walk back towards the station again.

Once the blue lights had passed I turned round and hurried back. The pizza box was sitting untouched on the steps. Like I said, I was looking forward to seeing the look on Corina's face when she took her first bite.

CHAPTER **14**

"You haven't asked," she said in the darkness.

"No," I said.

"Why not?"

"I suppose I'm just not a very inquisitive person."

"But you must be wondering. Father and son . . ."

"I assumed you'd tell me whatever you felt like telling me when you felt like it."

The bed creaked as Corina turned towards me. "What if I never said anything?"

"Then I'd never find out."

"I don't get you, Olav. Why did you want to save me? **Me?** You're so lovely, and I'm so despicable."

"You're not despicable."

"How would you know? You don't even want to ask about anything."

"I know that you're here with me now. That's enough for the time being."

"And later? Say you manage to get Daniel before he gets you. Say we get to Paris. Say we somehow manage to scrape enough money together to survive. You'll still be wondering who she is, this woman who could be her own stepson's lover. Because who could ever really trust someone like that? Such a talent for betrayal . . ."

"Corina," I said, reaching for the cigarettes. "If you're worried about what I'm wondering or not wondering, feel free to tell me. All I'm saying is that it's up to you."

She bit my upper arm gently. "Are you scared of what I might say, is that it? Are you scared I'll tell you I'm not the person you're hoping I might be?"

I fished out a cigarette, but couldn't find a lighter. "Listen. I'm someone who has chosen to earn their daily bread killing other people. I'm inclined to give people a bit of leeway when it comes to their actions and decisions."

"I don't believe you."

"What?"

"I don't believe you. I think you're just trying to hide it."

"Hide what?"

I heard her gulp. "That you love me."

I turned towards her.

The moonlight from the window sparkled in her moist eyes.

"You love me, you fool." She hit me limply on the shoulder. And repeated "You love me, you fool. You love me, you fool," until her eyes were streaming with tears.

Blood on Snow

I pulled her to me. Held her until my shoulder felt warm, then cold from her tears. Now I could see the lighter. It was on top of the empty red cardboard box. If I had been in any doubt, I knew now. She liked the CP Special. She liked me.

CHAPTER 15

The day before Christmas Eve.

It had got colder again. That was the end of the mild weather for the time being.

I called the travel agent's from the phone box on the corner. They told me what plane tickets to Paris would cost. I said I'd call back. Then I phoned the Fisherman.

I said without any preamble that I wanted money for fixing Hoffmann.

"We're on an open line, Olav."

"You're not being bugged," I said.

"How do you know?"

"Hoffmann pays a guy at the phone company who knows what phones are being bugged. Neither of you is on the list."

"I'm helping you sort out your problem, Olav. Why should I pay you for that?"

"Because you'll earn so much from Hoffmann being out of the way that this will be small change."

A pause. But not a long one.

"How much?"

"Forty thousand."

"Okay."

"In cash, to be picked up from the shop first thing tomorrow."

"Okay."

"One more thing. I'm not going to risk coming to the shop this evening—Hoffmann's people are getting a bit too close. Get the van to pick me up round the back of Bislett Stadium at seven o'clock."

"Okay."

"You got hold of the coffins and van?"

The Fisherman didn't answer.

"Sorry," I said. "I'm used to organising everything myself."

"Unless there was anything else?"

We hung up. I stood there looking at the phone. The Fisherman had agreed to forty thousand without a word of complaint. I'd have been happy with fifteen. Didn't the old shyster know that? It didn't make any sense. Okay, so it didn't make sense. I'd undersold myself. I should have asked for sixty. Eighty, maybe. But it was too late now; I'd just have to be happy with the fact that I'd actually managed to renegotiate the terms once.

As a rule I get nervous more than twenty-four hours before a job. And then I get less and less nervous as I start to count down the hours.

It was the same this time.

I stopped by the travel agent's and booked the Paris tickets. They recommended a small hotel in Montmartre. Reasonably priced, but cosy and romantic, the woman behind the counter said.

"Great," I said.

"A Christmas present?" The woman smiled as she typed in the booking under a name that was close to mine, but not quite the same. Not yet. I'd correct it just before we set off. She had her own name on a badge on the front of the pear-green jacket that was evidently the agency's uniform. Heavy make-up. Nicotine stains on her teeth. Suntan. Maybe subsidised trips to the sun were part of the job. I said I'd be back the following morning to pay in full.

I went out onto the street. Looked left and right. Longing for darkness.

On my way home I realised I was mimicking her. Maria.

Was. That. It.

"We can buy what you need in Paris," I said to Corina, who seemed considerably more nervous than I was.

By six o'clock I had dismantled, cleaned and oiled my pistol and put it back together. Filled the magazine. I showered and changed in the bathroom. Thought through what was about to happen. Thought that I'd have to make sure Klein was never behind me. I put my black suit on. Then sat down in the armchair. I was sweating. Corina was freezing.

"Good luck," she said.

"Thanks," I said, then got up and left.

CHAPTER 16

I stamped my feet on the slope in the darkness behind the old skating and football stadium.

It had said in the **Evening Post** that it was going
to be really cold that night and over the next few
days, and that the record was bound to be broken
now.

The black van pulled up at the edge of the pavement at exactly seven o'clock. Not a minute before,
and not a minute after. I took that as a good sign.

I opened the back door and jumped in. Klein
and the Dane were each sitting on a white coffin.
They were both wearing black suits, white shirts
and ties, as I had requested. The Dane welcomed
me with some funny remark in his guttural grunt
of a language, but Klein just glared. I sat down on
the third coffin and banged on the window of the
driver's cab. This evening's chauffeur was the young
guy who had noticed me when I first went into the
fishmonger's.

The road up to Ris Church wound through quiet

residential streets. I couldn't see them, but I knew what they were like.

I sniffed. Had the Fisherman used one of his own delivery vans? If he had, I hoped for his sake that he had put a fake number plate on it.

"Where's the van from?" I asked.

"It was parked in Ekeberg," the Dane said. "The Fisherman asked us to find something suitable for a funeral." He laughed out loud. "'Suitable for a funeral.'"

I dropped my follow-up question about why it stank of fish. I'd just realised that it was them. I remembered that I too had smelled of fish after my visit to the back room.

"How does it feel?" Klein suddenly asked. "Getting ready to fix your own boss?"

I knew that the less Klein and I said to each other, the better. "Don't know."

"Course you do. Well?"

"Forget it."

"No."

I could see that Klein wasn't going to let it go.

"First, Hoffmann isn't my boss. Second, I don't feel anything."

"Of course he's your boss!" I could hear the anger as a low rumble in his voice.

"If you say so."

"Why would he **not** be your boss?"

"It's not important."

"Come on, man. You want us to save your arse tonight, how about giving us"—he rubbed his thumb and forefinger together—"something in return?"

The van turned sharply and we slid around on the slippery coffin lids.

"Hoffmann paid for my services per unit," I said. "And that makes him my customer. Apart from that—"

"Customer?" Klein repeated. "And Mao was a **unit**?"

"If Mao was someone I fixed, then Mao was a unit. I'm sorry if that was someone you had an emotional attachment to."

"An emotional att—" Klein spluttered the words, then his voice cracked. He stopped and took a deep breath. "How long do you expect to live, then, fixer?"

"Tonight it's Hoffmann who's the unit," I said. "I suggest we try to focus on that."

"And when he's been fixed," Klein said, "some-one else will be the unit."

He stared at me without even trying to conceal his hatred.

"Seeing as how you evidently like having a boss," I said, "maybe I should remind you of the orders the Fisherman gave you."

Klein was about to raise his ugly shotgun, but the Dane put a hand on his arm. "Take it easy, Klein."

The van slowed down. The young man spoke through the glass. "Time to get in your vampire beds, boys."

We each lifted the lid of our diamond-shaped coffin and squeezed inside. I waited until I saw Klein lower the lid on his own coffin before lowering my own. We had two screws to fasten the lids from the inside. Just a couple of turns. Enough to hold them in place. But not so much that they couldn't be pushed off when the time came. I was no longer nervous. But my knees were trembling. Weird.

The van stopped, doors were opened and closed, and I could hear voices outside.

"Thanks for letting us use the crypt." The driver's voice.

"Not a problem."

"I was told I could have some help carrying them."

"Yes, don't suppose you'll get much help from the dead 'uns."

Gruff laughter. I reckoned we'd been met by one of the gravediggers. The back door of the van opened. I was closest to it, and felt myself being picked up. I lay as still as I could. Air holes had been drilled in the base and sides, and I could see beams of light in the darkness of the coffin as they carried me into the passageway.

"So this is the family that died on the Trondheim road?"

"Yes."

"Read about it in the paper. Tragic. They're being buried up north, aren't they?"

"Yes."

I could feel that we were going down, and I slid backwards, hitting my head against the end of the coffin. Shit, I thought they always carried coffins feetfirst.

"You haven't got time to drive them up before Christmas?"

"They're being buried in Narvik, that's a two-day drive." Little shuffling steps. We were in the narrow stone staircase now. I remembered it well.

"Why not send them up by plane?"

"Those concerned thought that was too expensive," the young man said. He was doing well. I'd told him that if there were too many questions he should say he'd only just started work at the funeral directors'.

"And they wanted them in a church in the meantime?"

"Yes. Christmas and all that."

The coffin levelled out again.

"Well, that's understandable. And there's plenty of room here, as you can see. Just that coffin there, being buried tomorrow. Yes, it's open, the family are due soon for a viewing. We can put this one on these trestles."

"We can put it straight on the floor."

"You want the coffin on the concrete floor?"

"Yes."

They'd stopped moving. It felt as if they were deliberating.

"Whatever you want."

I was put down. I heard a scraping sound by my head, then steps fading away.

I was alone. I peered through one of the holes. Not quite alone. Alone with the corpse. A unit. My corpse. I had been alone here last time as well. My mum had looked so small lying there in the coffin. Dried up. Maybe her soul had taken more room inside her than most people's do. Her family were there. I'd never seen them before. When my mum hooked up with my father, her parents had cut her off. The idea that someone in their family would marry a criminal wasn't something my grandparents, uncles and aunts could tolerate. That she had moved to the eastern side of the city with him was the only consolation: out of sight, out of mind. But I was in sight. In full sight of my grandparents, uncles and aunts, who up to then had only been people Mum had talked about when she was drunk or high. The first words I heard any of my relatives apart from my parents say to me were "so sorry." About twenty people saying how sorry they were, in a church on the west side of the city, just a stone's throw from where she grew up. Then I had withdrawn to my side of the river once more, and had never seen any of them again.

I checked that the screws were still in place.

The second coffin arrived.

The footsteps died away again. I looked at the time. Half past seven.

The third coffin arrived.

The driver and the gravedigger went away, their voices disappearing up the steps as they talked about Christmas food.

So far everything had gone according to plan.

The priest obviously hadn't objected when I called on behalf of the family in Narvik to ask if the church would mind having the three coffins in the crypt over Christmas while they were en route. We were in position, and, with a bit of luck, in half an hour Hoffmann would be here. We could always hope he'd leave his bodyguards outside. Either way, it was no exaggeration to say that the element of surprise would be entirely on our side.

The luminous dial of my watch swam and smouldered in the darkness.

Ten to.

On the hour.

Five past.

A thought struck me. Those sheets of paper. The letter. It was still under the cutlery tray. Why hadn't I got rid of it? Had I just forgotten? And why was I asking myself that, rather than **what if** Corina found it? Did I want her to find it? Anyone who knew the answers to questions like that would be a rich man.

I heard vehicles outside. Doors closing.

Footsteps on the staircase.

They were here.

"He looks peaceful," a woman's voice said quietly.

"They've made him look really nice," an older woman's voice sniffed.

A man's voice: "I left the car key in the ignition, I think I'll just go—"

"You're not going anywhere, Erik." The younger woman. "God, you're such a sissy."

"But my dear, the car—"

"It's parked in a churchyard, Erik! What do you think's going to happen to it here?"

I peered out of one of the holes by my side.

I had hoped that Daniel Hoffmann would come alone. There were four of them, and they were all standing on the same side of the coffin, facing me. A balding man, similar in age to Daniel. Not much like him. Brother-in-law, maybe. That fitted with the woman beside him: she was in her thirties, and there was a girl of ten or twelve. Younger sister and niece. There was a certain family resemblance. And the older, grey-haired woman was the spitting image of Daniel. Big sister? Young mother?

But no Daniel Hoffmann.

I tried to convince myself that he'd be coming in his own car, that it would have been odd for the whole family to turn up in the same vehicle.

This was confirmed when the brother-in-law with the receding hairline glanced at his watch.

"It was always the plan that Benjamin would

take over from his father," the older woman sniffed. "What's Daniel going to do now?"

"Mother," the younger woman said in a warning tone.

"Oh, don't pretend Erik doesn't know."

Erik raised and lowered the shoulders of his jacket, and rocked on his heels. "Yes, I know what Daniel's business entails."

"Then you know how ill he is as well."

"Elise has mentioned it, yes. But we don't have much to do with Daniel. Or this . . . er . . ."

"Corina," Elise said.

"Maybe it's time for you to see a bit more of him, then," the older woman said.

"Mother!"

"I'm just saying, we don't know how long we're going to have Daniel."

"We've got no intention of having anything to do with Daniel's business, Mother. Just look at what happened to Benjamin."

"Shh!"

Steps on the stairs.

Two figures came into the room.

One of them hugged the older woman. Nodded curtly to the younger one and the brother-in-law.

Daniel Hoffmann. And with him a Pine who was keeping his mouth shut for once.

They took up a position between us and the coffin, with their backs to us. Perfect. If I think a unit that I need to fix might be armed, I'll go to almost any lengths to get myself in a position where I can shoot them in the back.

I clenched my fist round the handle of the pistol.

Waiting.

Waiting for the guy in the bearskin hat.

He didn't come.

He must have been in position outside the church.

That would make things easier to start with, but he could be a potential problem that we'd have to deal with later.

My cue to the Dane and Klein was simple: when I yelled.

And there wasn't a single logical reason in the world why that shouldn't happen right then. But it still felt as if there was a right moment, one particular second squeezed in between all the other seconds. Like with the ski pole and my father. Like in a book, when an author decides precisely when something will happen, something you know is going to happen, because the author has already said it's going to happen, but it hasn't happened yet. Because there's a proper place in a story, so you have to wait a bit, so that things can happen in the right order. I closed my eyes and felt the clock count down, a spring tensing, a drop still clinging to the point of an icicle.

And then the moment arrived.

I yelled and pushed the lid off.

CHAPTER 17

I t was light. Light and cosy. Mum explained that I had a high temperature, and that the doctor who had been there said I had to stay in bed for a few days and drink a lot of water, but that there was nothing to worry about. That's when I could tell she was concerned. But I wasn't scared. I was fine. Even when I closed my eyes it was light, it was shining through my eyelids, a warm red glow. I had been put in Mum's big bed, and it felt as if all the seasons were passing through the room. Mild spring turning into scalding hot summer, with sweat running like summer rain from my forehead onto sheets that stuck to my thighs, then at last the relief of autumn, with clear air, clear senses. Until it was suddenly winter again, with chattering teeth and a long drift through sleep, dream and reality.

She had been to the library and taken out a book for me. **Les Misérables.** Victor Hugo. "Concise edition," it said on the cover, under a drawing of

Blood on Snow

Cosette as a young girl, the original illustration by Émile Bayard.

I read, and dreamed. Dreamed and read. Added and cut scenes. In the end I wasn't sure how much the author had come up with, and how much was my own invention.

I believed the story. I just didn't think Victor Hugo was telling it truthfully.

I didn't believe Jean Valjean had stolen bread, that that was why he had to make amends. I suspected that Victor Hugo didn't want to risk readers not cheering the hero on if he told the truth. Which was that Jean Valjean had killed someone. That he was a murderer. Jean Valjean was a good man, so the person he had killed must have deserved it. Yes, that was it. Jean Valjean had killed someone who had done something bad, and had to pay for it. The business about stealing bread just annoyed me. So I rewrote the story. I made it better.

So: Jean Valjean was a deadly killer who was wanted throughout France. And he was in love with Fantine, the poor prostitute. So in love that he was willing to do anything for her. Everything he did for her, he did out of love, madness, devotion, not to save his own immortal soul or out of love for his fellow man. He submitted to beauty. Yes, that's what he did. Submitted to and obeyed the beauty of this ruined, sick, dying prostitute with no teeth or hair. He saw beauty where no one could imagine it. And for that reason it was his alone. And he was its.

It took ten days for the fever to start to ease. For me it had felt like one day, and when I came back Mum sat on the edge of the bed, stroked my forehead, sobbed gently and told me how close it had been.

I told her I had been to a place that I wanted to go back to.

"No, you mustn't say that, Olav, darling!"

I could see what she was thinking. Because she had a place that she always wanted to go back to, where she would travel in a bottle.

"But I don't want to die, Mummy. I just want to make up stories."

CHAPTER 18

I was up on my knees, both hands on the pistol.

I saw Pine and Hoffmann spin round, almost in slow motion.

I shot Pine in the back, speeding up his pirouette. Two shots. White feathers leaped from his brown jacket, dancing in the air like snow. He had pulled his pistol free of his jacket and fired, but didn't manage to raise his arm. The bullets hit the floor and walls and ricocheted noisily around the stone room. From the corner of my eye I saw that Klein had got the lid off the coffin next to me, but hadn't yet climbed out. Perhaps he wasn't keen on the hail of bullets. The Dane had emerged from his coffin and had taken aim at Hoffmann, but because they'd put his coffin at the end of the crypt I was in his line of fire right behind Hoffmann. I jerked back at the same time as I swung my pistol towards Hoffmann. But he was surprisingly quick. He threw himself over the coffin, right at the young girl, and took her down with him as he landed by the long wall of the crypt, behind the rest of his family who were standing there like pillars of salt, mouths agape.

Pine was lying on the floor under the table Benjamin Hoffmann's coffin was on, his pistol hand sticking stiffly away from his body, like a dipstick he'd lost control of. It swung round, firing out bullets at random. Blood and spinal fluid on the concrete floor. A Glock pistol. Plenty of bullets. Just a matter of time before one of them hit someone. I put another bullet in Pine. And kicked at Klein's coffin as I raised the pistol towards Hoffmann again. I got him in the sights. He was sitting on the floor with his back against the wall and the young girl in his lap, holding her tight with one arm around her skinny ribcage. With the other hand he was aiming a pistol directly at her temple. She was sitting completely still, just looking at me with big brown eyes, not blinking.

"Erik . . ." It was the sister. She was looking at her brother, but talking to her husband.

And the man with the half bald head finally reacted. He took an unsteady step towards his brother-in-law.

"Don't come any closer, Erik," Hoffmann said. "These men aren't after you."

But Erik didn't stop, he carried on stumbling forward, like a zombie.

"Fuck!" the Dane yelled, shaking and hitting his

pistol. Obviously not working. A bullet had probably jammed. Bloody amateur.

"Erik!" Hoffmann repeated, aiming the pistol at his brother-in-law.

The father held out his arms towards his daughter. Moistened his lips. "Bettine . . ."

Hoffmann fired. The brother-in-law staggered back. Hit in the stomach.

"Come out, or I'll shoot the girl!" Hoffmann shouted.

I heard a deep sigh beside me. It was Klein, who had got to his feet and was aiming his sawn-off shotgun in front of him, towards Hoffmann. But the table and Hoffmann junior's coffin were in the way, so he had to take a step closer to the coffin to get a clear line of fire.

"Get back, or I'll shoot her!" Hoffmann was screaming in falsetto now.

The shotgun was pointing down, at an angle of about forty-five degrees, while Klein leaned back, away from the shotgun, as if he were afraid it was going to go off in his face.

"Klein," I said. "Don't do it!"

I saw him begin to close his eyes, the way you do when you know something's going to go off, but you don't know exactly when.

"Sir!" I shouted, trying to get eye contact with Hoffmann. "Sir! Let the girl go, please!"

Hoffmann stared at me as though to ask if I took him for a fool.

Damn. This wasn't how it was supposed to happen. I reached out and took a step towards Klein.

The blast from the shotgun rang in my ears. A cloud of smoke rose towards the ceiling. Short barrel, large spread.

The girl's white blouse was now covered in polka dots, one side of her neck was torn open, and Hoffmann's face looked like it was burning. But they were both alive. As Hoffmann's pistol skidded away across the floor, Klein leaned over the coffin on the table and stretched his arm out so that the barrel was against the girl's shoulder and the end reached Hoffmann's nose, as he tried desperately to hide behind her.

He fired again. The shot blew Hoffmann's face back into his head.

Klein turned to me with the excited face of a madman. "A unit! Was that enough of a unit for you, you bastard?"

I was ready to shoot Klein in the head if he raised the shotgun towards me, even if I knew it contained nothing but two empty cartridges now. I glanced at Hoffmann. His head was sunken in the middle, like a windfall apple that had rotted from within. He was fixed. So what? He would have died in the end. We all die in the end. But at least I had outlived him.

I got hold of the girl, grabbed the cashmere scarf from Hoffmann's neck and wound it round her neck, which was pumping out blood. She just stared at me with pupils that seemed to fill her whole eyes. She hadn't said a word. I sent the Dane over to the stairs to check that no one was coming while I got the grandmother to press her hand against the wound in her granddaughter's neck to stop the worst of the bleeding. From the corner of my eye I saw Klein reload that ugly gun of his with two new cartridges. I kept a firm grip on my pistol.

The sister was on her knees beside her husband, who was moaning in a low, monotonous voice, his hands folded over his stomach. I'd heard that getting gastric acid in a wound is agony, but I guessed he'd live. But the girl . . . Shit. What harm had she done anyone?

"What do we do now?" the Dane asked.

"We sit quietly and wait," I said.

Klein snorted. "What for? The pigs?"

"We wait until we hear a car start up and drive away," I said. I remembered the calm look of concentration beneath the bearskin cap. I could always hope he wasn't really that devoted to duty.

"The gravedigger has—"

"Shut up!"

Klein stared at me. The tip of the shotgun tilted upwards slightly. Until he noticed where my pistol was pointing, and lowered it again. And he shut up.

But someone else didn't. The voice came from under the table.

"Fuck, fuck, fuck, fucking bastard fucking hell . . ."

For a moment I thought that the guy was dead

but his mouth was refusing to stop, like the body of a snake chopped in half. I'd read that they could carry on wriggling for up to a day afterwards.

"Shit crap fucking bollocking bastard fucking cunt crap."

I squatted down beside him.

Where Pine had got his nickname was a subject of debate. Some people said it came from the Norwegian word for "pain," because he knew exactly where to cut his women if they didn't do their job, places that would cause more pain than disfigurement, and where the scars wouldn't damage the goods too much. Others said it was from the English word "pine," because he had such long legs. But right now it looked as if he would be taking his secret with him to the grave.

"Argh, shitting bastard cocksucker! Christ, it fucking hurts, Olav!"

"Doesn't look like it's likely to hurt much longer, Pine."

"No? Shit. Can you pass me my cig?"

I pulled the cigarette from behind his ear and stuck it between his trembling lips. It bobbed up and down, but he managed to keep hold of it.

"L-l-light?" he stammered.

"Sorry, I've given up."

"Sensible man. You'll live longer."

"No guarantee."

"No, course not. You m-might get hit by a b-b-bus tomorrow."

I nodded. "Who's waiting outside?"

"Looks like you're sweating, Olav. Warm clothes or stress?"

"Answer."

"And what do I get for t-t-telling you, then?"

"Ten million kroner, tax-free. Or a light for your cigarette. Your choice."

Pine laughed. Coughed. "Only the Russian. But he's good, I think. Career soldier, something like that. Don't know, poor sod doesn't talk much."

"Armed?"

"Christ, yes."

"What with? An automatic?"

"How are you getting on with that match?"

"Afterwards, Pine."

"Show a dying man some mercy, Olav." He coughed up some blood onto my white shirt. "You'll sleep better, you know."

"Like you slept better after you forced that deaf-mute girl to go on the streets to pay back her guy's debts?"

Pine blinked at me. The look in his eyes was weirdly clear, as if something had eased.

"Ah, her," he said quietly.

"Yes, her," I said.

"You must have m-m-misunderstood that one, Olav."

"Really?"

"Yes. She was the one who came to me. She **wanted** to repay his debts."

"She did?"

Pine nodded. It almost looked like he was feeling better. "I actually said no. I mean, she wasn't that pretty, and who wants to pay for a girl who can't hear what you want her to do? I only said yes because she insisted. Then, once she'd taken on the debt, it was hers, wasn't it?"

I didn't answer. I didn't have an answer. Someone had rewritten the story. My version was better.

"Oy, Dane!" I shouted over to the entrance. "Have you got a light?"

He moved his pistol to his left hand without taking his eyes off the steps as he fished out a lighter with his right hand. We're such weird creatures of habit. He tossed it to me. I caught it in the air. The rough scraping sound. I held the yellow flame to the cigarette. I waited for it to be sucked into the tobacco, but it carried on burning straight up. I held it there for a moment, then lifted my thumb. The lighter went out, the flame was gone.

I looked around. Blood and groaning. Everyone concentrating on their own business. All except Klein, who was concentrating on mine. I met his gaze.

"You go first," I said.

"Huh?"

"You go first up the steps."

"Why?"

"What do you want me to say? Because you've got a shotgun?"

"You can have the shotgun."

"That isn't why. Because I say you should go first. I don't want you behind me."

"What the fuck? Don't you trust me, then, or what?"

"I trust you enough to let you go first." I couldn't even be bothered to pretend that I wasn't pointing at him with the pistol. "Dane! Shift yourself. Klein's leaving."

Klein stared at me steadily. "I'll get you back for this, Johansen."

He kicked off his shoes, walked quickly over to the bottom of the stone steps and crept up them into the gloom, crouching as he went.

We peered after him. We saw him stop, then straighten up to take a quick look above the top step, then crouch down again at once. Evidently he hadn't seen anyone, because he stood up and carried on going, holding the shotgun in both hands at chest height, like it was a fucking Salvation Army guitar. He stopped at the top of the steps and turned back towards us, waving us up.

I held the Dane back as he made to follow him.

"Wait a moment," I whispered. Then started to count to ten.

The salvo of shots came before I got to two.

It hit Klein and threw him back over the edge of the stairs.

He landed halfway down and slid towards us, already so dead that his muscles weren't even spasming, as gravity pulled him from step to step like a freshly slaughtered carcass.

"Fucking hell," the Dane whispered, staring at the corpse as it stopped at our feet.

"Hello!" I called in English. The greeting bounced between the walls as if it were being answered. "Your boss is dead! Job is over! Go back to Russia! No one is going to pay for any more work here today!"

I waited. Whispered to the Dane to look for Pine's car keys. He brought them over and I threw them up the stairs.

"We are not coming out until we hear the car leaving!" I called.

Waited.

Then finally an answer in broken English: "I don't know boss is dead. Maybe prisoner. Give me boss, I will leave and you will live."

"He is very dead! Come down and see!"

He laughed, then said: "I want my boss come with me."

I looked at the Dane. "What do we do now?" he whispered, as if he were some sort of fucking chorus.

"We cut his head off," I said.

"What?"

"Go back in and cut Hoffmann's head off. Pine's got a serrated knife."

"Er . . . which Hoffmann?"

Was he a bit thick? "Daniel. His head is our ticket out of here, get it?"

Blood on Snow

I could tell he didn't get it. But at least he did as I asked.

I stood in the doorway keeping an eye on the stairs. I could hear quiet voices behind me. It seemed like everyone had calmed down so I took the opportunity to assess what I was thinking. As usual in stressful situations, it was a random mixture of odd things. Like the fact that the jacket of Klein's suit had twisted on the way down, so I could see from the label inside that it was hired, but it was now so full of bullet holes that they were unlikely to want it back. That it was very practical that Hoffmann's, Pine's, and Klein's corpses were already in a church and that there were spare coffins for each of them. That I'd booked seats on the plane just in front of the wings, with a window seat for Corina, so she'd be able to see Paris when we were coming in to land. Then a couple more useful thoughts. What was our van driver doing now? Was he still waiting for us on the road below the church? If he'd heard the shots, he would have heard that the last ones were from an automatic, which wasn't part of our arsenal. It's always bad news when the last shot you hear is the enemy's. His orders were clear, but could he keep a cool head? Had anyone else in the neighbourhood heard the shots? How did the gravedigger fit into all this? The job had taken much longer than planned. How much time did we have before we **had** to be out of there?

The Dane came back to the doorway. His face

was pale. But not as pale as the face of the head dangling from his hand. I checked that it was the right Hoffmann, then indicated that he should throw it up the stairs.

The Dane twisted the hair on the head a couple of times, took a short run-up, swung his arm by his side as though he was in a bowling alley, and let go. The head sailed upwards, hair flailing, but the angle was too tight and it hit the ceiling, fell onto the steps and bounced back down with little cracking sounds like when you tap a hard-boiled egg with a spoon.

"Just need to get my eye in," the Dane muttered as he grabbed the head again, shifted his feet, closed his eyes in concentration and took a few deep breaths. I realised I was on the edge mentally now, because I was about to burst out laughing. Then he opened his eyes, took two steps forward and swung his arm. Let go. Four and a half kilos of human head described a fine arc up to the top of the steps and hit the floor. We heard it bounce and roll down the passageway.

The Dane nudged me with a look of triumph, but managed not to say anything.

We waited. And waited.

Then we heard a car start. Revving. The gears crunched badly. Reversing. More revving. Far too much for first gear. It screamed off, driven by someone who wasn't used to driving it.

I looked at the Dane. He puffed his cheeks and

let out the air, shaking his right hand as if he'd been holding something hot.

I listened. Listened hard. It was like I could feel them before I heard them. Police sirens. The sound carried a long way in the cold air. It could still be a good while before they got here.

I glanced behind me. Saw the young girl in her grandmother's lap. It was impossible to say if she was breathing, but judging by the colour of her face she was drained of blood. I took in the whole room before I left. The family, death, blood. It reminded me of a picture. Three hyenas and a zebra with its stomach torn open.

CHAPTER 19

It's not true that I don't remember what I said to her on the train. I don't remember if I've said that I can't remember, but I certainly thought of saying it. But I do remember. I told her I loved her. Just to see how it felt to say it to someone. Like shooting at targets in the shape of human torsos; it's obviously not the same, but it still feels different from shooting at plain round targets. Obviously I didn't mean it, just as little as I meant to kill the torso-people on the targets. It was practice. Familiarisation. One day maybe I'd meet a woman I loved and who loved me, and then it would be good if the words didn't catch in my throat. Okay, so I hadn't actually **told** Corina that I loved her yet. Not out loud, like that, honestly, with no possibility of retreat, just going for it, letting the echo fill the vacuum, inflating the silence so much that it made the walls bulge. I had only said it to Maria at the exact point where the tracks met. Or divided. But the thought that I would soon be saying it to Corina made my heart feel like it was going to explode. Was I going to say it that evening? On the plane to Paris? At the hotel in Paris? Over dinner, perhaps? Yes, that would be perfect!

That was what I was thinking as the Dane and I walked out of the church and I breathed in the raw, cold winter air that still tastes of sea salt even when ice has settled on the fjord. The police sirens could be heard clearly now, but they came and went like a badly tuned radio, still so far off that it was impossible to tell which direction they were coming from.

I could see the headlights of the black van on the road below the church.

I was walking across the frozen path with short, quick steps, my knees slightly bent. That's something you learn as a child in Norway. Maybe not as early in Denmark—they don't have so much snow and ice—and I sensed that the Dane was falling behind. But that might not be true. Maybe the Dane had walked on more ice than I had. We know so little about each other. We see a nice round face and open smile, and hear cheerful Danish words that we don't always understand, but they soothe the ear, calm the nerves, and tell us a story of Danish sausages, Danish beer, Danish sunshine and the gentle, sedate life on the flat farmland way down south. And it's all so nice that it makes us lower our guard. But what did **I** know? Maybe the Dane had fixed more people than I ever would. And why did that thought pop up just then? Maybe because it suddenly felt like time was waiting for something again, another squeezed second, a spring coiled tight.

I was about to turn round, but never made it.

I couldn't blame him. After all—like I said—I'm usually willing to go to any lengths to be in a position to shoot an armed man in the back.

The shot echoed across the churchyard.

I felt the first bullet as pressure on my back, and the next like a jaw clamping hard round my thigh. He had aimed low, just as I had done with Benjamin. I fell forward. Hit my chin on the ice. I rolled over and stared up into the barrel of his pistol.

"Sorry, Olav," the Dane said, and I could tell he meant it. "It's nothing personal." He'd aimed low so he could tell me that.

"Smart move by the Fisherman," I whispered. "He knew I'd be keeping an eye on Klein, so he gave you the job."

"That's pretty much it, Olav."

"But why fix me?"

The Dane shrugged. The wailing police sirens were getting closer.

"The usual, I suppose," I said. "The boss doesn't want someone out there who's got something on him. That's worth bearing in mind. You have to know when to quit."

"That's not why, Olav."

"I know. The Fisherman's a boss, and bosses are scared of people who are prepared to fix their own bosses. They think they're next in line."

"That's not why, Olav."

"For fuck's sake, can't you see I'm bleeding to death here? How about we skip the guessing game?"

The Dane cleared his throat. "The Fisherman said you have to be a bloody cold businessman not to bear a grudge against someone who has fixed three of your men."

He took aim at me, his finger tightening round the trigger.

"Sure you haven't got a bullet jammed in the magazine?" I whispered.

He nodded.

"One last Christmas wish. Not in the face. Please, grant me that."

I saw the Dane hesitate. Then he nodded again. Lowered the pistol slightly. I closed my eyes. Heard the shots. Felt the projectiles smash into me. Two lead bullets. Aimed at where normal people have their heart.

CHAPTER 20

M y wife made it," he had said. "For the play."

Loops of metal, all hooked together. How many thousands of them could there be? Like I said, I thought I'd got something out of the exchange with the widow. A coat of chain mail. It's hardly surprising Pine had thought I looked sweaty. I was dressed up like a fucking medieval king under my suit and shirt.

The metal top had dealt fine with the shots to my back and chest. My thigh wasn't so fortunate.

I could feel the blood pumping out as I lay there motionless and watched the tail lights of the black van flare off into the night and disappear. Then I tried to stand up. I almost passed out, but managed to get to my feet, and staggered towards the Volvo that was parked in front of the church door. The chorus of sirens was getting closer with each passing second. There was at least one ambulance in the choir. The gravedigger must have worked out what was going on when he called them. Maybe they'd be able to save the girl. Maybe not. Maybe I'd be able to save myself, I thought as I yanked open the door of the Volvo. Maybe not.

But the brother-in-law had been telling the truth to his wife: he had left the key in the ignition.

I squeezed myself in behind the wheel and turned the key. The starter motor whined in complaint before giving up. Fuck, fuck. I let the key click back, then tried again. More whining. Start, for fuck's sake! If there's any point in making cars up here in this snowy shithole, surely it has to be that they start even if it's a few lousy degrees below freezing. I thumped the steering wheel with one hand. I could see the blue lights flare like the aurora borealis in the winter sky.

There! I put my foot down. I let go of the clutch and the wheel spun through the ice until the studded tyres got a grip and sent me swerving towards the churchyard gate.

I drove a couple of hundred metres down among the villas before turning the car round and heading back towards the church at a snail's pace. I'd hardly set off again before I saw the blue lights in the rearview mirror. I obediently signalled to pull over and turned into the driveway of one of the villas.

Two police cars and an ambulance went past. I could hear at least one more police car on its way, and waited. And realised that I had been here before.

Bloody hell. It was right in front of this house that I had fixed Benjamin Hoffmann.

There were Christmas decorations and plastic tubes that were supposed to look like candles in the living-room window. A sliver of cosy family life shone out onto the snowman in the garden. So the boy had managed it. Maybe he'd had some help from his father; maybe he used a bit of water. The snowman was properly done. Adorned with a hat, a blank stone grin, and stick arms that seemed to want to embrace the whole of this rotten world and all the crazy shit that happened in it.

The police car passed and I reversed out onto the road again and drove away.

Luckily there were no more police cars. No one to see the Volvo desperately trying to drive normally, but which still—without it quite being possible to put your finger on why—was being driven differently from all the other cars on the streets of Oslo on the day before Christmas Eve.

I parked right next to the phone box and turned off the engine. My trouser leg and the seat cover were soaked in blood, and it felt like I had some sort of evil heart in my thigh, pumping out black animal blood, sacrificial blood, satanic blood.

Corina widened her big blue eyes in horror when I opened the door of the flat and stood there swaying.

"Olav! Dear God, what happened?"

"It's done." I pushed the door shut behind me.

"He . . . he's dead?"

"Yes."

The room was slowly starting to spin. How much blood had I actually lost? Two litres? No, I'd read that we have five to six litres of blood, and pass out if we lose much more than twenty per cent. And that would be roughly . . . fuck. Less than two, at any rate.

I saw her case on the floor of the living room. She was packed and ready for Paris, the same things she had brought with her from her husband's flat. Former husband. I'd probably packed far too much. I'd never been farther than Sweden before. With my mum, that summer when I was fourteen. In the neighbour's car. In Gothenburg, just before we went into Liseberg amusement park, he had asked me if it was all right for him to hit on my mum. Mum and I took the train home the following day. Mum had patted me on the cheek and told me I was her knight, the only knight left in the whole world. The fact that I thought there was a false note in her voice was probably because I was so confused at the whole of this sick adult world. But, like I said, I'm completely tone-deaf; I've never been able to tell the difference between pure and false notes.

"What's that on your trousers, Olav, is it . . . blood? Oh God, you're hurt! What happened?" She looked so bewildered and upset standing there that

I nearly laughed. She gave me a suspicious, almost angry look. "What is it? Do you think it's funny that you're standing here bleeding like a stuck pig? Where've you been shot?"

"Only in the thigh."

"Only? If the artery was hit, you'll soon bleed out, Olav! Get those trousers off and sit down on the kitchen chair." She removed the coat she had been wearing when I came in and went into the bathroom.

Came out again with bandages, plasters, iodine, the whole shebang.

"I'll have to sew you up," she said.

"Okay," I said, leaning my head against the wall and closing my eyes.

She got going, trying to clean the wound and stop the bleeding. She made comments as she worked, explaining that she could only patch me up provisionally. That the bullet was still in there somewhere, but that it was impossible to do anything about that now.

"Where did you learn to do this?" I asked.

"Shh, just sit still, or you'll break the stitches."

"You're a proper little nurse."

"You're not the first man to get a bullet in him."

"Oh," I said, in a matter-of-fact way. As a statement, not a question. There was no rush, we'd have plenty of time for stories like that. I opened my eyes and looked down at the bun at the back of her head as she knelt in front of me. Breathing in her scent.

Blood on Snow

There was something different about it, something mixed in with the good smell of Corina close to me, Corina naked and passionate, Corina's sweat on my arm. Not much, but a hint of something, ammonia, maybe, something that almost wasn't there, but was there. Of course. It wasn't her, it was me. I could smell my own wound. I was already infected, I'd already started to rot.

"There," she said, biting off the end of the thread.

I stared down at her. Her blouse had slid off one shoulder and she had a bruise on the side of her neck. I hadn't noticed it before, it must be one Benjamin Hoffmann had given her. I felt like saying something to her, that it would never be allowed to happen again, that no one would ever lay a hand on her again. But it was the wrong time. You don't reassure a woman that she's safe with you while she's sitting there patching you up so you don't bleed to death in front of her.

She washed the blood away with a damp towel and wound a bandage round my thigh.

"It feels like you've got a temperature, Olav. You need to get to bed."

She pulled off my jacket and shirt. Stared at the chain mail. "What's that?"

"Iron."

She helped me off with it, then ran her fingers over the bruises left by the Dane's bullets. Loving. Fascinated. Kissed them. And as I lay in bed and felt the shakes come, and she wrapped the duvet around me, I felt just like before when I lay in Mum's bed. It almost didn't hurt any more. And it felt as if I could escape it all, but it wasn't up to me; I was a boat on a river, and the river was in charge. My fate, my destination was already determined. Which just left the journey, the time it took and the things you saw and experienced along the way. Life seems simple when you're sufficiently ill.

I slipped into a dream world.

She was carrying me over her shoulder, running as the water splashed around her feet. It was dark and there was a smell of sewage, infected wounds, ammonia and perfume. From the streets above us came the sound of shots and shouting, and streaks of light filtered through the holes in the drain covers. But she was unstoppable, brave and strong. Strong enough for both of us. And she knew the way out of here, because she'd been here before. That was how the story went. She stopped at a junction in the sewers, put me down, said she had to take a look around but would soon be back. And I lay there on my back, listening to the rats scampering about me as I stared up at the moon through a drain. Drops of water hung from the grid pattern up above, revolving, shimmering in the moonlight. Fat, red, shiny drops. They let go, hurtled down towards me. Hit me in the chest. Passed straight through the chain mail, to where my heart was. Warm, cold. Warm, cold. The smell . . .

• • •

I opened my eyes.

I said her name. No answer.

"Corina?"

I sat up in bed. My thigh was throbbing and aching. Laboriously I lowered my foot over the edge of the bed and switched on the light. Jumped up. My thigh had swollen so much it was almost creepy. It looked like it had just carried on bleeding, but all the blood had built up inside the skin and bandage.

In the moonlight I could see her case in the middle of the living-room floor. But her coat was gone from the chair. I got to my feet and limped over to the kitchen. I opened the drawer and lifted out the cutlery tray.

The sheets of paper were still there in their envelope, untouched.

I took the envelope over to the window. The thermometer on the outside of the glass showed that the temperature was still dropping.

I looked down.

There she was. She'd just gone out for a bit.

She was standing hunched in the phone box, with her shoulders facing the street, the receiver pressed to her ear.

I waved, even though I knew she couldn't see me. Christ, my thigh hurt!

Then she hung up. I took a step back from

the window so I wasn't standing in the light. She came out of the phone box and I saw her look up towards me. I stood completely still, and she did the same. A few snowflakes hung in the air. Then she started walking. Putting her feet down with her ankles straight, placing one foot close to the other. Like a tightrope-walker. She crossed the street back towards me. I could see footprints in the snow. Cat footprints. Rear feet in the same prints as the front ones. The thin light from the street lamps meant that the edge of each print cast a small shadow. No more than that. Just that . . .

When she crept back inside the flat I was in bed with my eyes closed.

She took her coat off. I had been hoping she might take the rest off as well and get into bed with me. Hold me for a while. Nothing else. Loose change counts as money. Because now I knew that she wouldn't come and carry me through the sewers. She wasn't going to rescue me. And we weren't going to Paris.

Instead of getting onto the bed, she sat on the chair in the dark.

She was watching. Waiting.

"Will it take him long to get here?" I asked.

I saw her jerk in the chair. "You're awake."

I repeated the question.

"Who, Olav?"

"The Fisherman."

"You're feverish, Olav. Try to get some sleep."

"That's who you were calling from the phone box just now."

"Olav . . ."

"I just want to know how long I've got."

She was sitting with her head bowed, so her face was in shadow. When she spoke again it was with a different, new voice. A harder voice. But even to my ears the notes sounded purer. "Twenty minutes, maybe."

"Okay."

"How did you know . . . ?"

"Ammonia. Skate."

"What?"

"The smell of ammonia, it sits in your skin after you've been in contact with skate, particularly before the fish has been prepared. I read somewhere that it's because skates store uric acid in their flesh, like sharks do. But what do I know?"

Corina looked at me with a distant smile. "I see."

Another pause.

"Olav?"

"Yes."

"It's nothing . . ."

"Personal?"

"Exactly."

I felt the stitches tear. A stench of inflammation and pus belched out. I put my hand on my thigh.

The gauze bandage was soaked. And it was still stretched tight—there was loads more to come out.

"So what is it, then?" I asked.

She sighed. "Does it matter?"

"I like stories," I said. "I've got twenty minutes."

"This isn't about you. It's about me."

"And what are you about, then?"

"Yes. What am I about?"

"Daniel Hoffmann was dying. You knew that, didn't you? And that Benjamin Hoffmann would be taking over?"

She shrugged. "You've pretty much got me there."

"Someone who deceives the people she needs to deceive without a guilty conscience in order to follow the money and power?"

Corina stood up abruptly and went over to the window. Looked down at the street. Lit a cigarette.

"Apart from the bit about the guilty conscience, that's more or less right," she said.

I listened. It was quiet. I realised that it was past midnight, that it was now Christmas Eve.

"You just gave him a call?" I asked.

"I went to his shop."

"And he agreed to see you?"

I could see the silhouette of her pout against the window as she exhaled the smoke. "He's a man. Just like all other men."

I thought about the shadows behind the frosted glass. The bruise on her neck. It was fresh. How blind can you be? The beatings. The submission. The humiliation. That was how she wanted it.

"The Fisherman's a married man. So what did he offer you?"

She shrugged. "Nothing. For the time being. But he will."

She was right. Beauty trumps everything.

"When you looked so shocked when I came home, it wasn't because I was wounded, but because I was alive."

"It was both. You mustn't think I don't have any feelings for you, Olav. You were a good lover." She let out a short laugh. "At first I didn't think you had it in you."

"Had what in me?"

She just smiled. Sucked hard on her cigarette. The tip glowed red in the semi-darkness over by the window. And I thought that if anyone down in the street looked up at that moment, they might think they were looking at a plastic tube trying to imitate cosy home life, happy families, a sense of Christmas. And they might imagine that the people up there had everything I wished I had. Up there they lived the sort of lives people **ought** to live. I don't know. I just know that that's what I would have been thinking.

"Had what?" I repeated.

"The dominant thing. My king."

"My king?"

"Yes." She laughed. "I thought I was going to have to stop you there for a while."

"What are you talking about?"

"This," she said, pulling her blouse down over her shoulder and pointing at the bruise.

"I didn't do that."

She stopped with the cigarette halfway to her mouth and looked at me suspiciously.

"You didn't? Do you think I did it myself?"

"It wasn't me, I'm telling you."

She laughed gently. "Come on, Olav, it's nothing to be ashamed of."

"I don't hit women."

"No, it was harder to get you to do that, I'll give you that. But you liked the strangling. After I got you going you **really** liked that."

"No!" I pressed my hands to my ears. I could see her lips moving, but couldn't hear anything. It wasn't worth hearing. Because that's not how the story went. It had never been like that.

But her mouth kept making shapes. Like a sea anemone, which I once learned has its mouth as its anus and vice versa. Why was she talking, what was it she wanted? What was it they all wanted? I was deaf and dumb now. I no longer had the equipment to interpret the sound waves which they, normal people, produced incessantly, waves crashing over the coral reef and then vanishing. I stared out at a world that made no sense, had no coherence, just people desperately living the life that each of us has been given, instinctively sating every sick desire, stifling our anxieties about loneliness and the death-throes that start as soon as we realise we're mortal. I knew what she meant. Was. That. It?

I grabbed my trousers from the chair by the bed and pulled them on. The fabric of one of the legs was stiff with blood and pus. I heaved myself out of bed and dragged my leg behind me across the floor.

Corina didn't move.

I leaned down over my shoes and felt a wave of nausea, but managed to pull them on. My coat. I had my passport and the tickets to Paris in the inside pocket.

"You won't get far," she said.

The keys to the Volvo were in my trouser pocket.

"Your wound has opened up, just look at yourself."

I opened the door and went out into the stairwell. I got hold of the handrail and heaved myself down using my lower arms, as I thought about the randy little male spider realising that visiting time was over just a bit too late.

By the time I got downstairs my shoe was already sloshing with blood.

I set off towards the car. Police sirens. They had been there the whole time. Like wolves howling in the distance around the snow-covered hills that surrounded Oslo. Rising, falling, sniffing out the scent of blood.

This time the Volvo started at once.

I knew where I was going, but it was as if the streets had lost their shape and direction, becoming gently swaying tentacles of a lion's mane jellyfish that I had to keep swerving to follow. It was hard to see where you were in this rubber city where nothing wanted to stay as it was. I saw a red light and braked. Tried to get my bearings. I must have nodded off, because I jumped when the lights changed and a car behind blew its horn. I put my foot down. Where was this, was I still in Oslo?

My mum never said anything about my father's murder. It was as if it had never happened. And that was fine with me. Then one day, four or five years later, when we were sitting at the kitchen table, she suddenly asked: "When do you think he'll come back?"

"Who?"

"Your father." She looked through me, past me with unfocused eyes. "He's been gone a long time. Wonder where he's been this time?"

"He's not coming back, Mum."

"Of course he is. He always comes back." She raised her glass again. "He's very fond of me, you know. And you."

"Mum, you helped me carry him . . ."

She put the glass down with a bang, spilling some of the gin.

"Oh," she said without any trace of emotion, fixing her gaze on me. "Anyone who took him from me would have to be a terrible person, don't you think?"

She wiped the glistening liquid from the table-cloth with one hand, then went on rubbing it, as if she were trying to erase something. I didn't know what to say. She had put together a story of her own. And I mine. I could hardly start diving into that lake up in Nittedal just to see whose version was more truthful. So I said nothing.

But the knowledge that she could love a man who treated her like that taught me just one thing about love.

No, actually.

It didn't.

It taught me **nothing** about love.

We never spoke about my father again after that.

I turned the wheel to follow the road, matching it as closely as I could, but it was as if it was trying to shake me off the whole time, swerving so that I and the car would hit a wall or one of the cars coming in the other direction, disappearing behind me with wailing horns that diminished in strength like an exhausted barrel organ.

I turned off to the right. Found myself in quieter streets. Fewer lights. Less traffic. Darkness was falling. And then it got completely dark.

I must have fainted and driven off the road. Not fast. I had hit my head on the windscreen but there was no damage, either to windscreen or head. And the lamp post that the radiator had buckled around wasn't even bent. But the engine had stopped. I turned the key in the ignition a few times, but it just complained with ever decreasing enthusiasm. I opened the car door and crawled out. I lay on my knees and elbows like a Muslim praying, with the fresh snow stinging the palms of my hands. I moved my hands together, trying to gather up the powdery snow. But powdery snow is just that. It's white and beautiful, but difficult to make anything enduring out of. It promises so much, but in the end everything you try to make collapses, crumbling between your fingers. I peered up and looked around to see where I'd driven.

Leaning on the car I got to my feet, then staggered over to the window. I pressed my face to the glass, which was lovely and cool against my burning forehead. The shelves and counters inside were bathed in a flickering half-light. I was too late, the shop was closed. Of course it was, it was the middle of the night. There was even a sign on the door saying they'd closed earlier than usual: "Closing at 17:00 on December 23 for stocktaking."

Taking stock. Of course. It was the day before Christmas Eve, after all. The end of a year. Perhaps it was time for that.

In the corner, beyond the short train of trolleys, there was a Christmas tree, mean and small. But it still demanded the title—it was a Christmas tree, no matter what.

I didn't know why I had driven here. I could have

driven to the hotel and got a room there. Right across the street from the man we had just fixed. Opposite the woman who had fixed me. No one would think of looking for me there. I had enough money for two nights. I could call the Fisherman in the morning and ask to have the rest of the fee paid into my bank account.

I heard myself laugh.

Felt a warm tear trickle down my cheek, saw it fall and burrow into the fresh snow.

Then another one. It just disappeared.

I caught sight of my knee. Blood was oozing out through the fabric of the trousers and dribbling down to settle on the snow with a skin of slime, like egg whites. I knew it would disappear. Melt down and vanish like my tears. But it just lay there, red and quivering. I felt my sweaty hair stick to the glass of the window. It's probably a bit late to mention it now, but in case I haven't said, I've got long, slightly lank, blond hair and a beard, I'm average height and I've got blue eyes. That's pretty much me. There's an advantage to having a lot of hair and a beard: if there are too many witnesses to a job, you have the potential to change your appearance quickly. And it was this potential to change quickly that I now felt freezing to the window, setting root, like part of that coral reef I keep going on about. Anyway. I wanted to become one with this window, to become glass, just like the invertebrate anemones in **Animal Kingdom 5: The Sea** actually **become** the coral reef they live on. And in the morning I would be able to watch Maria, watch her all day without her seeing me. Whisper whatever I liked to her. Call out, sing. My only wish just then was to disappear—maybe it was the only thing I had **ever** wanted. To disappear, like Mum drinking herself invisible with neat spirits. Rubbing it in until it erased her. Where was she now? I no longer remember. I hadn't been able to remember for a long time. It was odd, I could say where my father was, but where was my mother, the woman who had given me life and kept me alive? Was she really dead and buried at Ris Church? Or was she still out there somewhere? Obviously I knew, it was just a question of remembering.

I closed my eyes and rested my head against the window. Relaxed completely. So tired. I'd soon remember. Soon. . . .

Darkness came. The great darkness. Spreading out like a huge, black cloak, coming towards me to take me in its embrace.

It was so quiet that I could hear a soft clicking sound that seemed to be coming from the door beside me. Then I heard steps, familiar, limping steps, approaching. I didn't open my eyes. The footsteps stopped.

"Olav."

I didn't answer.

She came closer. I felt a hand on my arm. "What . . . Are . . . You . . . Doing . . . Here."

I opened my eyes. Stared into the glass, at the reflection of her standing behind me.

I opened my mouth, but couldn't speak.

"Are . . . You . . . Bleeding."

I nodded. How could she be here now, in the middle of the night?

Of course.

Stocktaking.

"Your . . . Car."

I formed my mouth and tongue to say "yes," but no sound came out.

She nodded, as if to say she understood, then lifted my arm and put it over her shoulder.

"Come."

I limped towards the car, leaning on her, on Maria. The strange thing was that I didn't notice her limp; it was as if it were gone. She got me into the passenger seat, then went round to the driver's side, where the door was still open. She leaned over me and ripped open the leg of my trousers, which tore without a sound. She took a bottle of mineral water from her bag, unscrewed it and poured water on my thigh.

"Bullet?"

I nodded and looked down. It didn't hurt any more, but the bullet hole looked like the mouth of a gaping fish. Maria had pulled off her scarf and told me to lift my leg. Then she tied the scarf tightly round it.

"Hold . . . Your . . . Fingers . . . Here . . . And . . . Press . . . Hard . . . On . . . The . . . Wound."

She turned the key, still in the ignition. The car started with a soft, amiable purr. She put it in reverse and backed away from the lamp post. Pulled out onto the road and drove.

"My . . . Uncle . . . Is . . . A . . . Surgeon . . . Marcel . . . Myriel."

Myriel. The same surname as the junkie. How could she and he have an uncle with the same . . . ?

"Not . . . At . . . The . . . Hospital." She looked across at me. "At . . . Mine."

I leaned back against the headrest. She wasn't talking like a deaf mute. It was odd and jerky, but not like someone who couldn't talk, more like someone . . .

"French," she said. "Sorry . . . But . . . I . . . Don't . . . Like . . . Talking . . . Norwegian." She laughed. "I . . . Prefer . . . To . . . Write . . . Always . . . Have . . . Done. As . . . A . . . Child . . . I . . . Just . . . Read. . . . Do . . . You . . . Like . . . Reading . . . Olav?"

A police car drove past with its blue light slowly rotating on the roof. I saw it disappear in the mirror. If they were looking for the Volvo, they weren't paying attention. Maybe they were after something else.

Her brother. The junkie had been her brother, not her boyfriend. Younger brother, presumably, that was why she had been prepared to sacrifice everything for him. But why hadn't the surgeon, their uncle, been able to help them back then, why had she had to . . . ? Well, enough of that. I could find out the rest and work out how it all fit together later. But for the time being she had turned up the heater and the warm air was making me so drowsy I had to concentrate hard not to just drift off.

"I . . . Think . . . You . . . Read . . . Olav . . . Because . . . You . . . Are . . . Like . . . A . . . Poet . . . It . . . Is . . . So . . . Beautiful . . . What . . . You . . . Say . . . When . . . We . . . Are . . . Underground."

Underground?

My eyes closed as it slowly dawned on me. She had been able to hear everything I said.

All those afternoons on the train, when I thought she was deaf, she had just stood there and let me talk. Day after day, pretending she couldn't hear or see me. As if it were a game. That was why she had reached for my hand in the shop—she thought she knew that I loved her. That the box of chocolates was the sign that I was finally ready to step from fantasy into reality. Could that be how it all fit together? Could I really have been so blind that I had thought she was deaf and dumb? Or had I seen it all along, and simply denied the fact that I actually knew?

Could it have been the case that I had been on my way here, to Maria Myriel, all along?

"I'm . . . Sure . . . Uncle . . . Can . . . Come . . . Tonight . . . And . . . If . . . It's . . . Okay . . . With . . .

You . . . There'll . . . Be . . . French . . . Christmas . . .
Food . . . Tomorrow . . . Goose . . . A . . . Bit . . .
Late . . . After . . . Christmas . . . Eve . . . Mass."

I put my hand in my inside pocket and found
the envelope. I held it out, still with my eyes closed.
I felt her take the envelope, pull over to the side of
the road, stop. I was so tired, so tired.

She began to read.

Reading the words I had bled onto the pages, the
words I had smashed up and rewritten to get the
right letters in the right place.

And they didn't feel dead at all. On the contrary,
they were alive. And true. So true that "I love you"
sounded like the only thing that could be said. So
alive that everyone who heard the words must have
been able to see him, the man writing about the girl
he went to visit every day, the girl sitting in a supermarket, the girl he loved, but wished he didn't love,
because he didn't want to love someone who was
just like him, imperfect, with faults and failings,
another self-sacrificing, pathetic slave to love, who
obediently read people's lips but never spoke herself,
who subordinated herself and found her reward in
that. But at the same time, he couldn't manage not
to love her. She was everything he wished he didn't
want. She was his own humiliation. And the best,
the most human, the most beautiful thing he knew.

I don't know much, Maria. Only two things,
really. One is that I don't know how I could

make someone like you happy, because I'm the sort of person who wrecks things, not one who creates life and meaning. The second thing I know is that I love you, Maria. And that's why I never came to dinner that time. Olav.

I heard the sob in her voice as she read the last sentences.

We sat there in silence. Even the police sirens had gone quiet. She sniffed. Then she spoke.

"You . . . Have . . . Made . . . Me . . . Happy . . . Now . . . Olav . . . This . . . Is . . . Enough . . . Don't . . . You . . . Get . . . It?"

I nodded and took a deep breath. I can die now, Mum, I thought. I don't need to make up any more stories. I can't make this story any better.

CHAPTER 21

I n spite of the extreme cold it snowed all night, and when the first people to get up in the morning darkness looked out across Oslo, the city had put on a soft, white blanket. Cars drove slowly through the snow, and people smiled as they edged their way round the clumps of ice on the pavement, because no one was in a rush—it was Christmas Eve, a time for peace and reflection.

On the radio they kept going on about the record-breaking cold and colder times ahead, and in the fishmonger's on Youngstorget they wrapped up their last kilos of cod and sang "Merry Christmas" with that strange Norwegian voice that makes everything sound so happy and good-natured no matter what the message.

Outside the church in Vinderen the tape of the police cordon was still fluttering while inside the priest discussed with the police how to perform the Christmas service when everyone began to arrive that afternoon.

Blood on Snow

At Rikshospitalet in the centre of Oslo the surgeon walked straight from the young girl in the operating theatre out into the corridor, pulled off his gloves and went up to the two women sitting there. He saw that the fear and desperation hadn't left their rigid faces, and realised that he had forgotten to take off his mask so they could see the smile on his face.

Maria Myriel walked up the hill from the underground station towards the supermarket. It would be a short day at work, they were due to close at two o'clock. And then it was Christmas Eve. Christmas Eve!

She was singing a song in her head. A song about seeing him again. She **knew** she'd see him again. She had known it from the day he had come to take her away with him from . . . From everything she didn't want to think about any more. His kind blue eyes behind his long blond hair. His straight, thin lips behind his bushy beard. And his hands. They were what she thought about most. More than other people did, but that was only natural. They were a man's hands, but nice. Large and slightly square, the way sculptors imagine heroic workers' hands. But they were hands she could imagine stroking her, holding her, patting her, comforting her. The way her hands would him. Every so often she felt scared at the strength of her own love. It was like a dammed-up stream, and she knew that there was only a tiny difference between bathing and drowning someone in love. But she wasn't worried about that any longer. Because he looked like he'd be able to receive, and not just give.

She could see a group of people gathered in front of the shop. And there was a police car there. Had there been a break-in?

No, just a collision from the look of it. There was a car with its front wrapped round a lamp post.

But as she got closer she saw that the crowd seemed more interested in the window than the car, so perhaps there had been a break-in after all. A policeman emerged from the crowd and walked over to the police car, pulled out a radio microphone and began to talk. She read his lips. "Dead," "bullet wound" and "the right Volvo."

Now another policeman was waving and ordering the crowd back, and as they moved she caught sight of a shape. At first she thought it was a snowman. But then she realised that was because he was covered in snow, that there was a man standing there, leaning against the window. He was being held up by the long blond hair and beard that had frozen to the glass. She didn't want to, but she moved closer. The policeman said something to her, and she pointed to her ears and mouth. Then she pointed to the shop and showed her name on her ID card. She had occasionally thought about changing it back to Maria Olsen, but had come to the conclusion that apart from the drug debt, the only thing he had left her was a

French name that sounded a bit more exciting than Olsen.

The policeman nodded and indicated that she could unlock the shop, but she didn't move.

The Christmas carol in her head had fallen silent.

She stared at him. It was as if he had grown a thin skin of ice, and under it were thin blue veins. Like a snowman that had soaked up blood. Beneath frosted eyelashes his broken gaze was staring into the shop. Staring at the place where she would soon be sitting. Sitting and tapping the prices of groceries into her till. Smiling at the customers, imagining who they were, what sort of lives they lived. And later, that evening, she would eat the chocolates he had given her.

The policeman reached inside the man's jacket, pulled out a wallet, opened it, took out a green driver's licence. But that wasn't what Maria was looking at. She was staring at the yellow envelope that had fallen out into the snow when the policeman pulled out the wallet. The lettering on the front was written in ornate, beautiful, almost feminine handwriting.

To Maria.

The policeman strode off towards the police car with the driving licence. Maria bent down, picked up the envelope. Put it in her pocket. No one seemed to have noticed. She looked at the place it had been lying. At the snow and the blood. So white. So red. So strangely beautiful. Like a king's robe.

A NOTE ABOUT THE AUTHOR

Jo Nesbø is a musician, songwriter, economist, as well as a writer. His Harry Hole novels include **The Leopard, Phantom, The Redeemer** and **The Snowman,** and he is also the author of several stand-alone novels and the Doctor Proctor series of children's books. He is the recipient of numerous awards including the Glass Key for best Nordic crime novel.

A NOTE ABOUT THE TRANSLATOR

Neil Smith majored in Scandinavian Studies at University College London and lived in Stockholm for several years. He now lives in Norfolk, England. His translations include books by Liza Marklund, Mons Kallentoft, Leif GW Persson, Marie Hermanson and Anders de la Motte.

LIKE WHAT YOU'VE READ?

If you enjoyed this large print edition of
BLOOD ON SNOW,
here are a few of Jo Nesbo's latest
bestsellers also available in large print.

The Son
(paperback)
978-0-8041-9452-5
($26.00)

Police
(paperback)
978-0-8041-9446-4
($26.00)

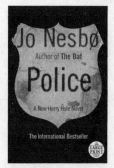

The Redeemer
(paperback)
978-0-8041-2108-8
($26.00)

Phantom
(paperback)
978-0-307-99081-5
($26.00)

Large print books are available wherever books
are sold and at many local libraries.

All prices are subject to change. Check with your
local retailer for current pricing and availability.
For more information on these and other large print titles,
visit www.randomhouse.com/largeprint.